To the memory
of
my Mother and Father,
my
first storytellers

By the same author:

At Slieve Gullion's Foot (Dundalgan Press, Dundalk)
Mountain Year (The Dolmen Press, Dublin)
Tyrone Folk Quest (Blackstaff Press, Belfast)

Plays

The Hard Man
Culprit Of The Shadows
Dust Under Our Feet
Men On The Wall
The Loughlin One
The Sell Out

NOW YOU'RE TALKING...

Folk Tales from the North of Ireland

Michael J. Murphy

Blackstaff Press

Published by Blackstaff Press Limited, 16 Donegall Square South, Belfast BT1 5JF with the assistance of the Arts Council of Northern Ireland.

SBN 85640 062 9 Cloth
SBN 85640 063 7 Paper

Printed by Belfast Litho Printers Limited.

CONTENTS

INTRODUCTION

Some of the tales presented here I have written down from memory, especially for this book, but most of them have been selected from the collections I have brought together during the past thirty years in the capacity of full-time collector for the Irish Folklore Commission and, latterly, for the Department of Irish Folklore, University College, Dublin, which succeeded the Commission in 1971.

The tales are all from an area sometimes referred to as 'Old Ulster', extending roughly from Rathlin Island in the North, and the Antrim coast, to the River Boyne in the south and from Strangford Lough in the east to Cavan in the west on the River Shannon. This area, consequently, includes Co Louth, now part of the Province of Leinster, as well as those Ulster counties forming part of the Republic of Ireland. I have not done any collecting in Co Donegal, however; this Ulster county has been thoroughly combed by my able colleague Sean O Heochaidh.

It has been my aim to make as representative a selection as possible of tales surviving in living oral tradition in this area. Most of the international folktale genres are represented, for instance Animal Tales, Tales of Magic, Religious Tales, Romantic Tales, and Jokes and Anecdotes. In addition examples of some genres of a more national or local nature have been included: hero tales about Finn McCool and his warriors, popular legends about Irish saints or other famous or infamous historical personalities, such as Daniel O'Connell, Dean Swift and the highwayman Redmond O'Hanlon, and, finally, legends concerned with supernatural beings and events. One sub-group within the last-mentioned category has been excluded: stories about the fairies. These are so numerous and so varied that it would be futile to attempt to give an idea of them within the limited scope of this small book.

On account of the lack of comparative studies between the tales of the north of Ireland and those found in other parts of the country, it would be premature to attempt to describe the special characteristics of the northern tradition. It would seem, however, that - with the exception of Donegal which occupies a special position because of the survival of the Irish language there - the North is especially rich in short, snappy humorous tales. The long Wonder Tales and the Hero Tales, so prominent wherever Irish is spoken, are only seldom met with and then only too often in truncated and confused versions. What is to be wondered at most, however, is not that such stories are in a state of decline as that they still survive at all. Neither are they lacking in charm, in spite of their shortcomings. And we ought to take pride in them, too, because they belong to *our* cultural heritage. Moreover, they are of great importance to the folklore scholar, since they provide invaluable links between Irish and Scottish tradition.

The collecting of tales and legends - as well as of other items of folklore - required, and requires, a studied and sensitive approach.

The storyteller could be shy: could be hesitant to trust a memory which hadn't heard or 'rehearsed' the tales for years because of the decay of the traditon. Furthermore, the quest itself and the occupation of folklore collecting were strange, and suspicions had to be allayed: people tended to suspect the collector of all kinds of secret missions - a Government agent keeping an eye on valid and invalid subsidies of one kind or another, a clerk who had absconded with the till, a schoolmaster hounded from his school, even a reolutionary on the run!

My background of country living in South Armagh aided me immensely. Before I took on folklore collecting as a job, and not the hobby it had been most of my life, I was a farm labourer and free-lance writer; I understood the work and crafts of the country-side, its manners and its vernacular.

I knew that a favourite starting point could be the blacksmith's forge. Most of these have now vanished; but the men often had to wait hours at the forge and there was an opportunity to talk and gossip. The smith, sometimes a storyteller himself, could verify and supplement one's assessment about this or that man who appeared to have the aptitude for folk storytelling. Or he could direct one to someone in the area known to have folklore and tales. He could also name houses where neighbours gathered at night to talk or 'crack' and tell tales; ordinary dwelling houses which we know in Ulster as '*céilí*-houses'. Once the Smith was assured of my good faith, I was recommended to use his name as an introduction.

As well as the blacksmith's forge, the cobbler's shop was another good source; these too have vanished from the countryside. I've also collected folklore and folktales in hospitals and in Homes for the Old People. Today, unless one has some prior contact in a fresh area, the pub is the usual starting point. The storyteller however is happier and more at ease when seated by his own or a neighbour's fireside where the mood is right. And it must be added that no storyteller was ever paid for his tales nor was payment expected.

I've met storytellers whose art was unknown in a locality and often unsuspected: so one keeps asking and making talk with any man or woman met on a road.

The storytellers were country people with normal occupations in the land or related crafts. Most of them were men, but I did find a few women storytellers. Among these was a representative of another vanished class known traditonally and romantically as 'The Travelling Woman'. She was a spinster or widow without a home or family ties; and while never designated as being a beggar-woman, roamed the countryside for miles and was welcomed warmly in the houses where she received food and shelter for the night on a make-shift bed in a corner of the kitchen close to the hearth.

The ages of most of my storytellers ranged from about sixty to over ninety years. Some were illiterate in the conventional sense, but all had a high degree of intelligence and good humour, as well as being gifted with excellent memories and fluent speech.

Until people got to know and accept the work of the folklore collector, all material had to be memorised and written down later; the sight of a notebook still alarms some people; while others frankly refuse to have their material taken down on tape. The tape recorder is now used throughout, whenever possible, but was unheard of in the early years of the work, although colleagues had used the cumbersome Ediphone. So that unless I was allowed to take down or type a story directly from the storyteller's narration, I had him repeat the tale later against my transcription.

I have aimed at the highest possible fidelity towards the speech of the storytellers, especially as far as vocabulary, grammar forms and syntax are concerned. A word of warning may not be out of place to those unfamiliar with northern Irish idioms: wherever forms like *come* are found where standard English would require *came* do not think that you have found a misprint!

These tales were told by grown-ups for grown-ups as most folk stories are. Strong language is part and parcel of the performance and could not have been cut out without destroying the particular flavour of folk speech. Tales taken from my manuscripts, consequently, appear exactly as they are found there with the following exceptions: (1) inadvertently skipped words have been silently supplied, spelling mistakes corrected and punctuation occasionally regularised, and (2) in two cases sentences containing statements about living persons that might have caused offence to them have been omitted.

Many of my informants are now dead; some of the houses where I sat night after night taking down or taping tales are now closed, or derelict, their hearths as cold as the heart of the storytellers in the clay of their graves. They loved to tell the tales and lamented the decay of the tradition, but were quietly delighted when the media of radio and television - even the motion-picture screen - took up themes and motifs from their stories.

It is my hope that these stories will provide as keen an enjoyment to their offspring, their friends and all my other readers as it did to them to tell them and to me to listen to them and collect them.

Acknowledgements

My special thanks are due to Professor Séamus Ó Duilearga under whose direction I worked for over thirty years. It was he who employed me as a collector, thus enabling me to direct my undivided attention towards the interest that lies closest to my heart.

I I am also deeply indebted to Professor Bo Almqvist, Head of the Department of Irish Folklore, University College, Dublin, for assistance and kind permission to publish this selection of folktales. The notes on the stories, p 156 - 176, are written by him.

My thanks are also due to Dr Caoimhin Ó Danachair of the Department of Irish Folklore who selected the photographs from the Archives of the Department.

Above all I pay homage and express my greatest indebtedness to the storytellers, living and dead, who told these tales with patience and fidelity to the oral tradition, often aware that their voice was the last to preserve this part of our national heritage in their own areas.

Michael J Murphy, Dromintee, South Armagh

A Toast

Here's to the top of the house
And the solid foundation;
The Hammers of Hell
And the Sledge of Damnation:
The curse of the priest
And the congregation
On any ould hag
That'll refuse me the daughter.

From Co Armagh

1 CONFESSION TALES

The storytellers: Mickey Joe Anderson and his wife

1. 'Anchor There'

The hard-case Roman Catholic seaman had been neglecting his religious duties for many years. A missionary priest persuaded him to return to Confession, which eventually he did, to another priest.

'How long,' asked the priest, 'since your last Confession?'

The penitent said it was years.

'Would it be two years?' asked the priest.

'Sail on,' says the penitent.

'Five years?'

'Sail on.'

'Not ten years?'

'Sail on.'

'Good Lord ... Twenty years?'

'Anchor there,' says the sailor.

2. Peas as Penance

Penitents at Confession when guilty of serious sin were ordered to make a pilgrimage with peas in their shoes.

Two men, neighbours, had been given such a penance in Confession: to walk from their homes to a distant church or Holy Well. Both set out together; but one man soon out-paced the other hobbling only quarter-ways.

In agony the sufferer asked how he did it: did he not put any peas in his boots?

'I did,' his neighbour replied; 'but I boiled them first.'

3. 'Two Days Running and Skip One'

There was these two country women, a sort of hard cases; and whatever the divil they were up to they were afeared to go to Confession to their own priest and made it up to go Confession one Saturday night in the town.

In the town this Saturday; and who the hell did they happen to go to but the toughest priest in it. One of the women was a deal younger than the other and she went in first and he kept her a helluva time. When she come out the other woman took her aside and asked her what he was like, that he'd kept her a very long time.

She said he was bad and not so bad - meaning the penance he'd given her.

'For,' says she, 'I'm to have two days running and skip one.'

In goes the other woman, made her Confession and got Absolution and it come to the penance, and says she to the priest:

'Try and be azy on me, Father,' she says, 'for I haven't the wind for running now and I'm too stiff to skip.'

4. 'Who Made Me?'

Another time in Dromintee there come a new priest to the parish and, begging his robes and the hands of the anointed, he was very short and gruff with the people: would stand no nonsense at all. He'd refuse you Absolution for the least slip.

There was a *caltherer* of a fellow in the parish then; worse, a fellow not like another - innocent. The old priest knew him well and knew he'd never spent a week at school and that anything he tried to learn went in one ear and out the other.

This Saturday he went to Confession and went to the same box he always went to, and who was in it but the new priest. There was only this red cloth, a curtain, between you and the people waiting to be heard. The fellow could never make his Confession right, but the new priest didn't know that. Anyway he stopped your man making his Confession and says he to him:

'Wait ... Wait. Who made you?'

'I don't know,' says your man.

'Get out,' says the priest. 'And don't you come back till you know what I've asked you.'

The *caltherer* done as he was bid and went outside the chapel. 'Who made me?' says he to himself. 'The only one would know that would be the oldest man in the parish. I'll ask him the morra.'

The next day, Sunday, he button-holed the oldest man in the parish coming from Mass. Told his story. The old man listened, knew well who he had, and he knew that if he told this fellow the answer he wouldn't remember it as far as the door.

'I'll have to think,' says the old man. 'But let you be at Confession with the same priest next Saturday. I'm going too and I'll be right behind you. When the priest asks you "Who made you?" I'll be there and I'll whisper the answer to you. That way you can't forget and you'll be all right and get Absolution.'

That was fair enough. Saturday night come and the *caltherer* went to Confession, and good enough the old man was there on the seat along the wall at the Confession-box right behind him. It come this fellow's turn to go in and make his Confession, and the old man leaned over and cocked his ear agin the curtain.

'So it's you?' says the priest. 'Well, who made you? Answer me.'

And at that the old man whipped a big darning needle out of the collar of his coat and through the curtain gives him a good jab of the needle in the arse.

'Aw Holy God of Almighty!' shouts this fellow when the needle went into him. 'Holy Merciful Christ of Almighty ...'

'Wheest ... Wheesht,' says the priest. 'That's enough.'

The fellow kept "Holy Godin' " so much that the priest give him Absolution right away and let him go.

5. A Bag of Begods

There was another fellow not quite as bad as the *caltherer* and it seems he went to the same priest; or one like him. He was making his Confession anyhow and said he had two main sins to confess. So the priest asked him how many times he would commit these sins since his last Confession. The fellow said he didn't know.

'You'll have to know,' says the priest, 'or I can't give you Absolution. What do you work at?' asks the priest.

'I'm a plough-man for the landlord,' says he.

'Have you any sacks in the field?' asks the priest.

He was no way short of bags and sacks.

'Well,' says the priest, 'when you find you've committed one of those sins put a wee stone in one sack; and when you find you've committed one of the other sins put a wee stone in another sack. Come back next Saturday night.'

Saturday night come. Well, in them times the chapel for Confession would be lit with a few candles: two at the door on every side aisle and maybe two near the altar rails. The chapel was full anyway when the priest heard this woeful commotion, someone banging and staggering agin the seats like a drunk man. He put his head out of the Confession-box to demand what was wrong, and here he sees this fellow with a full bag like a sack of priddies on his back. He dumped the bag down agin the Confession-box and says he:

'It's only me, Father. There's the bag of Begods an' Be-Jazes. I have the other bag of whore's getts out in an ass's cart at the gate.'

6. He Stole a Bit of Old Rope

This man went into Confession and told the priest he'd stolen a bit of old rope.

'What about that?' says the priest. 'That was nothing.'

'But, Father,' says he, 'there was a pig at the end of it.'

7. The Man Who Stole a Ham

Another man on tramp called at the parochial house for help and the door was open, and in the kitchen he seen six or seven hams hanging up a-curing. The priest's girl wasn't about. So he says:

'I could have a right tightener of a feed on one of them. What do they want with all them hams anyway.'

So he whips one and away. Going past the chapel he seen the people going into Confession, and stealing the ham sort of bothered him, so he goes in and in to Confession to the priest.

Makes his Confession and then he says:

'Father? Would you take a ham?'

'What would I be doing with a ham?' says the priest, 'I have more than enough at home.'

'I stole it, Father,' says he.

'Then you'll have to make restitution,' says the priest, 'and give it back to the man you stole it off.'

'I offered it to him and he wouldn't take it,' says the man.

'Oh, in that case you may keep it,' says the priest.

2 TALES OF PRIEST AND PARSON

The storytellers: Michael Rooney

8. In the Dark

Were you ever up at the Long Woman's Grave ... In the mountains between here and Omeath? Well this was supposed to happen up there. But it must be donkeys years and years ago, for there's not the track of a house there now.

Anyhow this old woman lived up there, her and her man called John, their two selves by their lone. And this day anyhow she was herding a cow or a calf on the road and they had sheep of course. When who comes walking up the road but this student—damn me if I can say for truth now whether he was going on for a priest or a parson, but one or the other. He got talking to this old woman anyhow and says she:

'Would you be a hatter from County Down come to buy wool?'

He said not; he said he was going on for a clergyman ... Damnbut I mind now he was going on for a priest. For he smelt bacon frying above in her house. Says he to her:

'Do you know what day it is?'

'Why,' says she, 'what day do you make it?'

'Friday,' says he, 'and yous are frying bacon. Do you not know that Christ died for you on a Friday?'

'And do you tell me,' says she, 'that that Man's dead? Sure up here John or me never hears a thing.'

'Dear me,' says this student, 'but yous're very much in the dark up here.'

'We are in troth,' says she, 'since the calf put his head through the window. John had to hang a bag in it.'

He give her a book or a leaflet and told her to try and read it and have it ready when he'd come back the next year.

'Why,' says she, 'what's it for?'

'To show you the light,' says he.

'Does that mean,' says she, 'you're going to put in a window for us?'

'Dear Oh dear,' says he. 'Do you know who made you?'

'Who made the world?' says she back.

Well, that was right enough. Says he next:

'And how many Gods are there then?'

'How many heads on a spade?' says she.

That was good enough too. Says he then:

'And how many Persons are there in God?'

'How many feet on a pot?' says she.

That was good enough too: she was only giving him tit for tat but he didn't know that. Three.

But when he come back the following year and met her herding he asked her if she'd read the leaflet, and she said she had.

'Well then,' says he, 'say it for me.'

'Sheep of God,' says she and he cut in:

'No, no: Lamb of God.'

'That was last year,' says she. 'A lamb would be a sheep the year.'

So he had to give her up. She was still in the dark.

9. The Priest to be Silenced

He was a Father Pat and he lived somewhere round Faughart. I never heard him talked of as only Father Pat. He was going to be silenced anyway for taking a drop too much: fond of the drink.

There was a conference to be held on him down in Armagh and the bishop and all the clergy were gathered to silence Father Pat: I don't know but it was a bishop the name of McGilligan was in it at the time.

Father Pat went to Armagh anyway and he was late arriving at the bishop's house where the conference was to be held, and when he went in there was no room left for him to hang up his coat and hat. It was a great day in summer and the sunbeam was shining through the window across the room. And whatever servant was there said he would have to put Father Pat's coat somewhere else.

'It's all right there,' says Father Pat and he threw the coat across the sunbeam and left it hanging there.

He was a man with great power you see.

Anyway Father Pat was put into this room be hisself; and there was a full five-naggin bottle of whiskey standing on the table and glasses and all. In about half an hour or so this curate come in to the room. Father Pat takes hold of the whiskey bottle and a glass and says he to this curate:

'Take a drop ' ... It was half empty by then.

'I never taste it,' says the curate.

'Take a drop, man,' says Father Pat. He filled a glass anyway and made the curate drink it. And it was wine now, not whiskey at all. So the curate went back and told what had happened, and Father Pat was brought into the conference and the bishop took the whiskey ... it was still like whiskey understand ... and he tasted it and it was wine. So he seen what had happened. And he says to Father Pat:

'God has given you power and I'll never take it off you.'

And that was that. Father Pat come back and was never silenced.

10. The Dog That Wouldn't Eat Meat on a Friday

A man has a dog which he claims will refuse to eat meat on a Friday. A wager is made and the meat laid out, and when put to the test as the dog goes for the meat the owner calls out:

'Friday! Friday!'

The dog immediately left the meat and walked over to its owner and he won his bet. But he didn't disclose that the dog's name was 'Friday'.

The man who lost the wager then claims that he has a cat which will not touch a live mouse. Another wager is made and he is challenged to prove his claim. A live mouse is nailed by the tail on a table: the cat is set at the opposite end of the table. But the cat doesn't move and the man wins his wager in return.

Neither does he disclose that his cat is blind!

11. The Dead Priest Speaks

The woman that told me this is dead and rotten this many a year and I wouldn't put a lie on her, God rest her, and she was never the sort to put a lie on anyone else. If I'm not mistaken it happened to her own mother the time she was the servant girl for a while with the priest in Jonesboro when they took over the barracks for the priest, the old barracks.

It was her job at night to close the chapel door. Now there's one would tell you she had a drop taken ... I wouldn't heed that, though Jonesboro had a Fair at the time and half-a-dozen public houses ... sort of sheebeens ... and all gone now.

But she was more than late this night closing the chapel and God save us when she went in, here she seen two candles lit on the High Altar for Mass. So she wondered and stood where she was at the door. And then she seen a strange priest come out and him in black vestments and he come as far as the altar rails and says:

'Is there anyone there fit to answer Mass?'

She said the flesh crept on her, for she'd never laid eyes on this priest before. And he asked three times if there was anyone fit to answer Mass, and at that he turned and went up and blew out the candles and went in to the vestry.

I don't think she waited to close the chapel that night but cleared like hell for home to the parochial house and whether the priest was up or not told him all she'd seen, what had happened.

Nothing would do him but she'd turn back and go with him to the chapel at once. She was afeared, but she went and they went into the chapel and there was nothing wrong he could see, and they closed the door and went home.

Next morning after Mass the parish priest says to her:

'Don't you mention a word of what you seen or heard to a living soul, but you be ready to come with me,' he says, 'to the chapel the night at the same hour.'

So she had to go. And they went and knelt at the back of the chapel and they had the doors closed. And at this hour out comes this priest and lit the candles.

'Is that the same priest?' says the parish priest.

'It is,' says she.

'Don't you speak for your life,' says he.

The strange priest come out with the black vestments on him and come as far as the altar rails and says:

'Is there anyone there fit to answer Mass?'

The priest kneeling beside her never opened his mouth and she didn't speak - maybe she wasn't fit anyway.

'Is there anyone there fit to answer Mass?' says this strange priest again.

Still the priest didn't make him an answer. And says the strange priest again:

'Is there anyone there fit to answer Mass?'

'Yes,' says the parish priest, 'I'm here.'

And he riz and went up and answered the Mass for this strange priest.

He was a priest that undertook to say a Mass and neglected it and he couldn't get into Heaven until it was said. He said he'd been coming at the self-same hour to the chapel for I don't know how long asking was there anyone there to answer Mass.

'I don't know how long,' says he, 'but do you know that big old hawthorn bush at the head of Quinn's Hill? Well, the bird dropped the haw for the quick for that bush when I first come out here.'

That was supposed to happen in Jonesboro: Ballincla was the old name for that place.

12. Old Thorns and Old Priests are to be Feared

Old thorns and old priests should be left alone: there's power in the pair of them if they want to use it. You may not believe it, but there was a time in Ireland when everyone believed it and maybe right they were. It's better be sure than sorry.

Anyhow, there was this fellow one time and he was very fond of the drink. Worse still he had a wife and a family, and the way he was drinking himself out of house and habitation they were living on the clippings of tin, licking the stones. She was sick, sore and tired scolding him and asking him to have sense, so in the latter end she went to the old parish priest about him.

The parish priest listened to her story and said he would see what he could do. So this day there was a market or something in the village and the priest knew your man would be there and wouldn't leave the public house till he lowered every cent in his pocket down the red lane, and maybe rise more on the slate if his name was good.

So the priest was in the village and he seen your man heading for the public house. He called him over.

'I forbid you to go in there this day,' says he.

'Only one drink, Father,' says he, 'and then I'm going home to my wife and childer.'

'One drink,' says the priest, 'will lead to another drink and another and another till you go home with the two legs plaiting under you. Now listen here,' says the priest, 'I don't want to use my power, but if you go inside that public-house today or let drink wet your lips - I'll turn you into a mouse by twelve o'clock tonight.'

At that the priest turned and walked away home, and your man turned and walked home too: he didn't want to draw the anger of the priest on him and he believed he had the power when he wanted.

He wasn't far outside the village on his way home and who does he meet but an old pal who'd been years in England or America and was just home. Well, you know how it is. Handshakes and great talk and what not: and before your man knew where he was, he was back with this pal in the pub in the village and didn't leave it till he couldn't see a hole in a ladder.

It was dark, down night when he got as far as his own house and his wife, Mary, was sitting lamenting to herself at the fire. He staggered in and looked at the mantelpiece and he could see the clock all right but he was that cross-eyed with drink he couldn't tell what time it was.

'Mary,' says he, 'what time is it?'

'What time do you think?' says she. 'It's a few minutes off midnight.'

'Mary,' says he, 'if you see me getting wee and hairy ... put out that bluddy cat.'

13. The Power of the Priest

During a deluge a priest under his umbrella rushed into a low thatched house where an old man and woman lived. They had never seen an umbrella before. The priest left down the umbrella to drip inside the door. They chatted, the shower passed and brilliant sunshine came out; the priest left to go, forgetting his umbrella.

When he had gone the old couple saw the umbrella. They were unable to get it through the narrow door. In the end the old man ran after the priest and called to him:

'Father? You forgot your wee house and we can't get it out the door.'

The priest returned, let down the umbrella, folded it, and left. The old man says to his wife:

'See that? Isn't the power of the priest great?'

14. For the Good of Her Ass

During the Great Famine when proselytism was fairly rife a minister approached an old woman to change her religion. He had found her grazing her donkey along the road. In return he agreed to afford her grazing for her donkey on the lands of The Glebe.

A few Sundays later the parson noticed the old woman leaving the Roman Catholic Church following Mass, and then later she attended his own service. He reproved her for this dualism of devotion and asked her to explain her conduct. She replied:

'Your reverence, I go to Mass first for the good of my soul, and then to your service for the good of me ass.'

15. The Greedy Priest and the Tramp

A miserly, greedy parish priest refuses to allow his house-keeper to assist any beggar or tramp who calls at the parochial house.

One day a tramp calls and asks to see the parish priest. The house-keeper reminds him that the priest will not see him and that she has been ordered to refuse any such help. The tramp says that he wants to ask the parish priest 'what he should do with a purse of gold found on a road'.

The house-keeper informs the priest who immediately directs her to bring the tramp to him. She does so. A fine meal is then set before the tramp who eats his fill. He is given a drink. Then the priest asks him to tell why he has called.

The tramp repeats his story: what he should do with a purse of gold found on the road?

The priest says:

'Bring it instantly to me. Where is it?'

'I haven't found any yet,' replies the tramp, 'but as soon as I do I'll bring it to you.'

16. 'It Died a Protestant'

The priest and parson ministering in the same parish were great friends. The minister also had some veterinary knowledge.

The priest's horse took sick and the minister was attending to it. A travelling man named Ward used visit both men and was always welcomed.

Ward called one day on the minister, who asked him how was the priest's horse.

'He's dead,' says Ward.
'Did he anoint him before he died?' says the minister.
'No,' replied Ward; 'he let him die a Protestant.'

3 SERVANT AND MASTER

The storytellers: Michael Murphy ('Mickey Buck', my father), right, with my wife Alice and myself

17. The Three Questions

It was this codger and he was hired as a herdsboy to a Bishop. Things were bad in Ireland at the time: the enemy had come and conquered the country and took the land and was killing all before them, priest and people.

So this evening the herdsboy come home and he seen the Bishop walking up and down and looking very down-in-the-mouth.

'My Lord Bishop,' says the herdsboy, 'what ails you? You look very down-hearted?'

'I'm to die in the morning,' says the Bishop.

'How is that?' says the herdsboy.

'I'm to lose me head,' says the Bishop. 'The chief that took over this country,' he says, 'sent for me this morning and give me three questions to answer by the morra morning and if I'm not fit he's to take the head off me.'

'What's the three questions, my lord?' says the herdsboy. 'I might be fit to help.'

'You could not,' says the Bishop. 'You might only lose your own head as well.'

Anyway he got the Bishop to tell him, and the herdsboy said that he would go in place of the Bishop next morning and to leave all to him.

'You'll only lose your head, too,' says the Bishop.

Morning come and the herdsboy set off and meets this big fella and stands before him.

'Who are you?' says he.

'I'm herdsboy to the Lord Bishop,' says he.

'Why didn't he come himself?' says he.

'The Lord Bishop didn't think it worth his while,' says he, 'to come himself to answer three simple questions.'

'Then if you're not fit to answer them you'll lose your head,' says this big fella.

'Fair enough,' says the herdsboy.

'Here's my first question then,' says the big fella. 'What's the first thing I think of in the morning when I rise?'

'What you'll ate,' says the herdsboy.

'That's right,' says he. 'Now here's me second question: How many loads of sand are there round the shores of Ireland?'

'One,' says the herdsboy, 'if you had a cart big enough to hold it.'

'Right,' says the big fella. 'And now here's my third and last question: How much am I worth?'

'Twenty-nine pieces of silver,' says the herdsboy.

'How do you make that out?'

'Well, Our Lord God Himself was sold for thirty pieces,' says the herdsboy, 'and you can't be as good as Him.'

And he got him and the Bishop off.

18. Three Things God Can't Do

The catechism says that God's fit to do anything; but there's three things He can't do:

He can't catch a baldy man by the hair of the head: He can't make two hills without a hollow: and He can't rise and give His seat to a better man.

19. The Wee Red Moiley

This lad one time took a notion he'd get better money if he hired across in Scotland and he crossed over and was hired by this Scotch farmer to herd sheep and cattle. So when he got to the farmer's place the farmer wanted to test him: whatever part of Ireland he was from he'd never seen mountain sheep in his life, the black faced horny sheep. So the farmer says:

'I'm going to test you whether you're worth your keep or not. Away like hell up that braeside and take down my flock of sheep here to the house. I'll give you such and such'n a time to have them down,' says the farmer.

Away goes the boy, and he was a long time away: a hellishin long time and the farmer was waiting.

'This playboy won't suit,' he'd say. And he went into the house. No sign of the boy with the sheep.

At long last the boy arrives and him drowned in his own sweat.

'What in hell kept you?' says the farmer. 'Where's the sheep?'

'Out in the shed,' says the lad.

'What kept you so long?'

'I managed the black-faces all right,' says the boy, 'but that wee red bugger of a moiley give me an awful lot of trouble.'

'What wee red bugger of a moiley?' says the farmer.

'Come out and see,' says the boy.

And he went out. And it was a big Scotch hare ...! He had him in the shed too, along with the horny sheep ...!

20. The Breed of the Old Mare

It was supposed to be a cuddy of a lad from The Glens here in Antrim was hired with this old woman away up by Loughguile. And every morning he'd waken up more tired than when he went to bed and he couldn't understand it. That went on for a while, and he was still tired every morning, and he happened to mention it to some old man was about that country. Says the old man to him:

'The woman you're working for is a witch,' says he. 'And every night that you go to bed she has a charm; she says some words and turns you into a wee horse and takes you out and rides you all round the country at whatever carry-on she be's at.'

So he told the lad what to do.

'Listen well the night,' says he, 'and whatever words she says - you say them about her as quick as you can and see what happens.'

Night come and the lad was in bed and let on to be asleep, and here good enough the old woman come and she had a wand or a bit of a stick and she started to say these words, and once he had them off, he says them agin her. And begod she turned into a mare. And he rode her all round the country and rode her home.

But what the old man didn't tell him was how he was to find out what words to say to change the mare back into the old woman: he didn't know and never got to know.

And there was ones round here at Cushendall would tell you the breed of that mare's about Loughguile yet ...!

21. 'I Won't Lay a Tooth on Her'

This lad was hired half time with two brothers that had land running into other: he'd work three days with one brother and the rest with the other: Sunday work too in them days.

Anyway, there was a lump of a pig tried to jump a barred

gate and hung itself. So it was all right: they butchered it and shared it out among the two houses and ate it. A while after that a calf got its head stuck in an old cart-wheel in a shed and choked itself and it was butchered and shared and they ate that.

There was the old mother in one of the houses and she took bad and died and the wee lad cleared home. It was a terrible thing then to leave your place and his father says:

'What took you home?'

'The old woman's dead,' says the lad, 'and I won't lay a tooth on her.'

He thought they'd have to ate her too ...!

22. A Hungry Hired Boy

This old man, he was getting very old, and he had a young wife; and she used to say to him every day:

'John,' she would say, 'you should get some man to help you to do a spot of work, because you're getting old.'

And they had no family.

'I might, I might: some day I might go into the village of a Fair day and hire a boy if I could get a man.'

So he went into the Fair anyway, and he searched through the whole Fair, and he could see nobody suitable in the whole Fair. So he was just about on his way home and he went in to this public house for a bottle of Guinness. And he seen a likely-looking young fellow standing about a couple of yards down the bar.

'Well,' he says, 'that's a fine young fellow.'

And he moved down and he says:

'There'd be no chance,' he says, 'that you'd be a young man looking for work?'

'Well,' says he, 'I'm in the Fair all day and no man asked me would you hire me. I'll definitely hire with you surely. I'm short of a few quid and I'll definitely hire with you.'

They made a bargain there and then.

'We'll have another couple of bottles of stout.'

So, he had a horse and trap. So they filed off and home; and when he came home - Aw, sure, the wife was all delighted, all lit up.

'Well, that's a great job, John. You brought a young man to

do a bit of work ... a spot of work for you. You're getting old, and sure you're not able to do it yourself. Well, I'm delighted that you have a young man.'

Well, there was cattle ... there was cows to be foddered and cows to be milked. The young fellow and him went out and they foddered the cattle and they done the whole work, out in the farm yard. When they came back in again she had two big blue duck-eggs for John and for the young fellow. And she had a big fadge cake in the press and she took it out, sawed it up and had a great big heap of bread on the table.

So, John went out to do something else, to give a calf a drink or something.

'Now,' she says to the young fellow, she says, 'we have no family. And only one bed. And if you wouldn't mind you could share the bed with me and John.'

'Wouldn't I sleep in an ould chair there at the fire; it'll do me rightly for the night.'

'Throt you'll not sleep at the fire: if you don't mind you'll share the bed with me and John.'

'I don't mind where I sleep for the night.'

'All right.'

John came back in, when he had the calf fed, or whatever he was doing. So when ten o'clock came they all filed into bed. The young fellow went in at the wall, and John in the centre, and her ladyship out at the stalk. And some time in the middle of the night a cow give a big loo [low] in the byre.

'Go down, John, quick,' she says, 'for there's a cow or something ... There's something wrong. There's a cow going to calve.'

'Will I bring the young fella?'

'Let the poor fella alone; he might be tired. Leave him where he is. If there's anything wrong you can come back for him.'

So John put on his trousers, threw a coat on him and went down to the byre: there was a cow sick a-calving. And he hadn't the latch gone off the door when she tipped the young fellow.

'John is gone down to the byre to see a cow.'

'Will I go down with him?'

'Stay where you are. You're all right, stay where you are.'

'John ... Would John be long away in the byre?'

'He ... He'll be long enough; the byre's a good bit from the house.'

'Would he be ten minutes?'

'He'll be long enough.'

'Do you think ... would he be fifteen minutes?'

'Won't he be long enough?'

'God, I'm going to do something ...'

'Ah, well do it quick,' she says, 'whatever you're going to do.'

'Bejasus I'll go down to the kitchen for another slice of thon ould cake. I'm starving with hunger.'

23. 'Go On With the Funeral'

Of five brothers in a family one was bone-lazy. The four brothers, migrating from Ireland to the English harvest, took him along so that he would be compelled to work or starve. Again he refused to work.

They decided to bury him in an old cemetery; and with him lying on a door the four brothers were carrying him to a live burial. An English farmer on the way asked them who was dead.

'He's not dead,' said one brother; 'but he won't work and we're going to bury him.'

'Oh, tha can't do that here,' says the English farmer. 'I'll give him wheat so that he can live.'

The brother on the door put up his head and asked was the wheat ground.

'Oh no,' says the English farmer; 'you'll have to do that yourself.'

The lazy brother lay down again on the door and says:

'Go on with the funeral, boys.'

24. A Boy Named Abraham

A boy named Abraham has been hired as a servant to a parson in the countryside. His work around the yard one Sunday morning takes longer than usual. Before he hurries off to church the cook hands him some pancakes. He hasn't time to eat them all and sticks the remainder inside his shirt front.

As he enters the church the parson is preaching. He is saying:

'Abraham, Abraham, what hast thou in thy bosom?'
'Pancakes, you hungry whore you.'

25. 'How Do You Like Your Egg Boiled'

A man has hired with a miserly woman and is beginning the first morning of his six month term. She says to him at breakfast:

'How would you like your egg boiled?'

'Along with another one,' says he.

'Right,' she says; 'I'll boil it in the tin along with my own.'

She allows the egg to boil hard. She says:

'Did I boil your egg too hard?'

'Never mind,' says he; 'I'll soften it with butter.'

Next morning she takes care that the egg is boiled on the soft side. She says:

'Did I boil your egg too soft?'

'Never mind,' says he; 'I'll harden it with butter.'

4 HUSBAND AND WIFE TALES

The storytellers: Dan Rooney

26. The 'Dead' Husband Returns

This is an incident that happened some years ago and it's supposed to be true. The man's name was Gilmartin and he got married. And after a couple of years his wife died and left him with one child, a baby girl.

So he decided after a couple of years to marry again. I don't think the second wife was as nice as the first, because when the little girl grew up the step-mother couldn't bear her, she was constantly fighting with her. So the father - when she was sixteen or a little older - the father used to leave home to fish; there was a lake right beside the house: to get away from the noise of his wife and daughter.

So this day he was fishing anyway and this young fellow was passing by the road with four head of cattle. So he asked the man that was fishing at the lake would he have a match. So the man come out where he was in the water fishing, he give him the match all right; and he says - he asked him where he was going?

He said he was going up above Manorhamilton in county Leitrim to a farm that his father owned, and that his father was giving him this farm of land because his step-mother - his father was married twice - the step-mother and him wasn't agreeing. So they decided that he go to live on this farm above Manorhamilton.

'It's the same thing,' says the man, 'is happening in our house. I'm married secondly,' he says, 'and my daughter and my second wife cannot agree. I'm nearly off my head,' he says, 'listening to them day after day fighting. That's what has me fishing in the lake.'

So he says:

'Could it be possible if you'd marry my daughter, and I'd give you four or five head of cattle and a little money? You can go into the house now and light your pipe and see her, see for yourself, and if you like her you'll get the cattle and the money.'

So the young fellow went in anyway to light his pipe, and he took a few glances at the girl and thought her lovely. So he came back out to where the man was fishing; and the man says:

'What do you think of her?'

'Well,' he says, 'I'd marry her if she hadn't the clothes to her back. I want no cattle,' he says, 'nor I want no money, if she marries me.'

'Well,' the man says, 'come back in to the house.'

So they went back in to the house, the young fellow and the man, and they got introductions to each other and told the whole situation. God, she give in to marrying him, because he was a fine-looking boy and so was she a fine-looking girl.

So anyway they went on to Manorhamilton; the house was fixed up and they lived there. After twelve months the man was fishing, and didn't a messenger come to the old man where he was fishing that his daughter was very sick in Manorhamilton hospital; a confinement case, going to have a baby, but she wasn't expected to live.

He was so fond of his daughter he started off, never put on a shoe, left the old shoes there, threw the rod into the lake. He got shoes in Manorhamilton, went into the hospital, and there he stayed the whole night with his daughter; and his own wife missed him then, that he wasn't coming in.

So she went to the lake; she got the shoes on the shore; the fishing rod was floating about on the water; and she come to the decision that Johnny was drowned.

So begod the hub-bub riz anyway and the neighbours was got and the police was got, and the lake was dragged. They got an old fiddler that was in the district was a-missing and was lost, in the lake. They got his body anyway and they put a sheet round it and brought him in, and the woman had a wake on him, and the neighbours come.

Two days after, coming back from the funeral, she started to cry: What would she do now that Johnny was dead? So this neighbour man says to her - he was an old bachelor:

'What would you do only marry again.'

'Ah,' says she, 'would I get anyone?'

'Aw, God, sure,' says he, 'I'll marry you if you'll marry me.'

'Come on to the house,' she says.

They come to the house anyways, and there was a little drink left over after the funeral and the two of them started to drink. So the woman, she says:

'You could stay here the night.'

'Aw well,' he says, 'I wouldn't like to stay.'

'Well,' she says, 'maybe we better go and get married secretly. We'll go down to the priest and sure no one will know it. Sure you can stay here then, it'll be no sin, no harm.'

So they went down to the priest anyway and the priest didn't like it at all, after burying the husband that day that she'd be out for marrying again. So he asked had he any money to give him, and he says:

'No.'

She says:

'There's a pig above at the house.'

That she'd give the priest the pig. So anyway the priest's servant-boy prepared to go for the pig, and had a rope and all. And in the meantime the man come from Manorhamilton. The daughter was after coming all right, there was a baby boy born, and he went in by the house. He didn't know what was wrong. He looked in on the window and seen butts of whiskey bottles and everything. He didn't know what happened.

He couldn't get in to his own house, it was locked; so he went in to the pig-sty where the pig was and he lay down in old bedding that was for the pig. And the next thing the priest's boy came in and put the rope on the pig, to bring the pig to the priest, and the squeals of the pig wakened your man and he jumped up.

The next thing the priest's boy made off; he seen the ghost of the man that was buried that day, and went back to the priest, and no pig.

He told them. So they wouldn't go home anyway, and she wouldn't go back; she believed the servant-boy that he did see the apparition.

That was Saturday night anyway. So Sunday morning your man that was after coming from Manorhamilton hospital struck for Mass early in the morning. Begod the people going to Mass looked behind and they seen him coming, the ghost, and they started to run. He says to himself:

'Begod I must be late. Look't, they're all running.'

And the quicker he run the quicker they disappeared from him. So he went into the chapel, and when he went in to the chapel they broke their neck across the altar rails, out through the sacristy. And the priest got all scared up after having interred the remains the day before that; and he asked him in the Name of God what took him back, or what was wrong?

'What's wrong with yous?' he says up.

The priest says:

'Didn't we bury you yesterday?'

'How would you bury me and me in Manorhamilton hospital

with my daughter?'

So the priest beckoned the people to come back and up, and he told the whole story. So the man that was supposed to marry her he disappeared out of the country and went to England. And your man and the wife lived happy after above Manorhamilton.

27. 'I Wish Death Would Take Me'

There was this old man and he was married to a young woman and they weren't hitting at all well: maybe he was jealous. She started to give him a sore time of it anyway, and maybe you couldn't blame her. He was no match for her, and he would sit all day in the ashes moaning and groaning to himself and saying he wished Death would come and take him.

There used to be *ceili*ers in the house, young fellows full of divilment, and they heard him and seen what was happening. So this night they thought to play a trick.

They got a rooster and they plucked him alive, as clean as your palm, and one of the young fellows went up on the roof with the rooster. The old boy was in the ashes below - it was a low thatched house: you could damn near put down your hand down the chimney and take the latch off the door.

He waited till he heard the old man groaning and moaning, and the young wife scolding him.

'I wish Death would come and take me,' says he.

At that the young fellow up on the roof let the rooster down the chimney. It lit in the *greesha* behind the fire and was all soot and not a feather on it. And it come stepping out from behind the fire.

The old fellow nearly died.

'Death,' he says, 'take her' - pointing to his wife. 'Take her, Death.'

28. A Desperate Falling Out

This man and his wife had a desperate falling out; and she mustn't have cared a helluva lot for him, for he said he would drown himself in the Newry Canal at Fathom and she agreed to help him.

He got her to tie his hands behind his back, and he stood on the brow of the Canal and told her to stand well back and take a running-race and give him a good dunt of her head in the small of his back. She said she would.

So she stood well back; but he was keeping an eye over his shoulder, and when she give this race and was about to give him the dunt of her head in the back - he stood aside and in she went, head first into the Canal. She come up yelling for him to save her.

'How can I save you?' says he: 'didn't you yourself tie me hands behind me back?'

29. The Travelling Woman and the Sowans*

It was this woman and she was married, but wasn't she carrying on with another man unknownst of the husband. He had his suspicions; and this time anyhow didn't he catch them, this man and his own wife, and there was holy blue murder.

There was an old Travelling Woman used to be going round the country: the Travelling Woman would get tea and a night in the house. She come in. She seen there was something up and she asked the woman of the house was there anything the matter.

'Oh,' says she, 'an awful unlucky job happened this morning.' Telling her what happened.

'Ah well, no matter,' says the Travelling Woman, 'I think I know a way of curing that. Leave it to me,' she says, 'But let this be a lesson to you.'

They had sowans for their supper that night: sowans made out of the oatmeal seeds. The Travelling Woman ate a great big bowl of these sowans. Dossed down in the corner and went to sleep. Next morning she asked the woman where her man was.

'He's away out in a temper working in thon field along the road,' she says.

Off goes the Travelling Woman and she sees him working like mad in the field beside the ditch; he was in a very bad humour. The Travelling Woman put her hand to her eyes to look at him and she says out hard:

'Good morra to the both of yous.'

'What do you mean?' says he, mad as hell. 'There's only me.'

'Aw,' says the Travelling Woman, 'I had a great big bowl of sowans for me supper last night and there's a great mist over me eyes. I'm seeing double.'

'Begod,' says he, 'I had sowans for me supper the other night too.'

* A type of gruel made from the husks of oats.

30. Beyond Redemption

It was during the time they burned kelp on the Island [Rathlin]: the whole Island would be hidden in the smoke of the kelp fires and one time a ship run ashore in it.

But that's not my story. Kelp-burning was wild thirsty work, and everyone helped and you had to keep the fire and the kelp turning night and day. The women helped to be sure, and this woman was fond of a drop and with the kelp burning got a drop too much. She was on her way home anyway and she fell unconscious drunk and lay there.

The boys working at this big kiln, getting it ready, saw her. They lit the kiln of kelp and carried her up and laid her alongside of it. She woke sometime during the night and the tongue thick in her head, and saw all the smoke and the fire and these fellows with long iron rods and everyone of them as black as the divils of hell.

'Where am I?' she says.

'You're in hell,' says this fellow. 'Don't you know you died in drink?'

She reached somehow into her skirt and took out some money.

She says: 'You likely know this place better nor me. Get me a drink - I'm wild dry and have a helluva sore head.'

31. A Divil's Imp of a Woman

She was a proper Divil's imp of a woman - always scolding or something - but she died anyway and the husband was heart glad. And lost no time about wake or funeral but wanted her buried right away: he couldn't get shut of her quick enough.

So the day of the funeral - it was a narrow, twisty lane from the house - they were carrying the coffin, and getting round this corner they knocked the coffin agin this gable-end; and the ones carrying it thought they heerd or felt a rattling in the coffin and they left it down.

They took off the lid and begod she was alive; only in a trance the whole time, and of course she be to be taken back to the house. She come to all right: and then hell and the Divil took her altogether ... The Divil never took her till then: because he buried her so quick.

But she died in the end that day twelve month and she was waked and all. And when they were carrying the coffin round the bend at this gable the husband says:

'Aw, boys, keep well away out from the gable at that corner.'

32. The Woman has the Last Word

It was a tailor they said from somewhere near here at Raholp or away be Saul maybe. And he got married, and he was in bed with the wife this morning and says he till her:

'Isn't it lovely to hear that thrush singing?'

'That's a blackbird,' says she.

'It's a thrush ...'

'It's a blackbird ...'

They never quit till they fell out about it. And that time twelve month they were in bed again and says she:

'Do you mind the lovely blackbird was singing this time last year?'

'That was a thrush,' says he.

'It was a blackbird ...'

'It was a thrush ...'

They fell out again; and they fell out every year over the same thing. Till in the latter end the tailor got old and his scissors wouldn't clip. The school-children got to know it and used to be jibing him about it: 'His old scissors won't clip!' And the wife started to say the same to him every time they'd fall out about the thrush and the blackbird.

'If you don't quit,' says he, 'I'll put your head in a gullion of water.'

'Old scissors won't clip,' says she.

So he takes her and puts her head under this gullion of water.

'Now will you shout "Old scissors won't clip"?' says he.

She was damn near dead by this time, but she put up her fingers and she done that with them, like scissors clipping. And died. But she had the last word.

33a. Courtship and Marriage

It was one of those country courtships which had gone on half a life time. Eventually the girl said to her lover:

'Do you know what they're saying about us?'

He asked what was being said.

'They're saying,' says she, 'that you and me is going to get married.'

'Man,' says he, 'won't we give them the quare gunk. Sure who'd take either of us at our time of day?'

33b.

The match had been made without the knowledge of the girl, which wasn't too unusual. One morning the girl's mother handed her good clothes and said:

'Get them on and put your smart ways about you.'

'Why,' says the daughter, 'what's up?'

The mother retorted:

'You're going to be married, that's what's up.'

'To who, Ma?'

'Never you mind who; it's none of your business,' replied the mother.

33c.

A girl and a man got married.

When they were married he was three times as old as the girl: when they were fifteen years married he was only twice as old. What age were they when they got married?

The girl was fifteen years of age and he was forty-five.

34. Pigs Can Go Under a Big Pot

This fellow went to Newry one day and bought two suckers [small pigs] and he was carrying them home. He fell in with a girl he knew and she'd bought a pot and was carrying it home. He had the suckers and she had the pot: and she said till him that she was afeared of him. He asked for why she was afeared of him.

'Amn't I carrying two suckers?' says he. 'What could I do? I can't leave down the suckers ...' [To court her].

'You can put them under the pots,' says she. [Suggestively: that he do so].

35. 'More Cake or I'll Appear'

Two sisters had invited two boys to the house and had prepared a fine meal for them. But they had a fool of a brother, and to keep him out of the way put him up in a garret with a currant cake.

The two boys arrived and the meal began and they were being very impressed. Suddenly the fool in the garret put his head out and cried:

'More cake or I'll appear.'

5 THE CLEVER AND THE FOOLISH

The storytellers: Peadar Barry, right

36. The Clever Man and the Fool

There was a man here in County Down one time and he left for Newry with the horse - there was no carts for a horse like now: slide-cars or wheel-cars or whatever it was. And he had no pockets to keep his money in either: the money was all in sovereigns and half-sovereigns at the time. It be to be a helluva time ago. Anyway, where did he put the money he had to buy things thinking to keep it safe? He hid the money in the mats [the straw matting under creel or bardocks straps] on the horse's back. He got to Newry and bought corn anyway; he put the horse in a stable in Newry of course. He went to pay for the corn, and when he went to get the money, the horse had straw and mats and money and all ate.

So what did he do? He took the horse out of the stable into the yard in Newry and stood with him till the horse started to dung. And then the man started hoking among the balls of dung; and he'd pick up a half-sovereign and put it away safe. He'd hoke again and he'd get another half-sovereign or a sovereign and put it away safe.

Well, this fool of a man was standing by in the yard watching: it was the man he'd bought the corn off and the fool of a man was waiting to get paid for the corn, and he seen all that was going on.

'That's a useful horse,' says the fool. 'Does he always dung like that?'

'He does to be sure,' says this man, the clever man. 'Jasus sure,' says he, 'what'd I do only for him.'

'Would you sell him?' says the fool of a man.

'I might,' says he.

He was an old horse you understand.

'Does he do that every day?' says the fool of a man.

'Sure only he does I wouldn't keep him,' says the other man.

And begod he sold the old horse to the fool of a man and got a helluva brave good price for him. And of course if the fool of a man was waiting till now he wouldn't find half a sovereign in the horse's dung. He had him at his own home by this time. And says he to his own wife:

'He'll not do me. I'll get my money back off him some way.'

The man that sold the fool the horse knew he'd be coming looking for his money one day: so him and his own wife made a plan. His wife had to have a big pot of broth on the fire, making broth with a sheep's head, mutton anyway. He sayed to his own wife that this fellow would likely soon be coming looking for his money over the old horse, but he said not to mind. And he goes and gets a bleddy big stone and takes it in to the house to have it ready. He says to the wife:

'Put that stone in the fire under the pot when you see him coming.'

And he cleared to keep out of the way. The pot was hanging on the crook, and when she seen this man coming she threw the big stone on the fire. The man comes in.

'Where's the good man here?' he says.

'He's out there somewhere,' she says.

And she looked in the pot and give it a stir and it was still boiling and she sipped it and said the broth must be done. The fool of a man said that that be to be a great stone would boil a pot of broth like that, and she said it was a great saving on coals.

'Would you sell it?' says he.

And he bought the stone and took it with him. The stone was nothing only an ordinary stone, and when he seen that at home the fool of a man got angered.

'I'm going surely to get my money the day,' he says.

So this man that sold the horse to him and the stone, he had two hares and he had them in a cage at the house. So he told the wife what she was to do when this fool of a man come again for his money. When the man come looking his money she was to tell him that her own man was down by the shore, three miles away gathering wrack, and she was to let on to send one of the hares for him to tell him to come home.

'If you shout or whistle or blow a horn or anything,' says he to his wife, 'I'll have your bleddy life.'

So good enough the fool of a man come looking his money and he says to her: 'Where's the good man the day?'

'He's down by the shore,' says she, 'but this hare here will soon bring him home. He'll take a message.'

So she let on to pet the hare and tell it the message and she let it out and away like hell went the hare.

'That's a great hare,' says this fool of a man.

'Oh,' says she, 'sure he's far better nor a servant-boy or girl for taking a message.'

And so sure her own man knowed about when to come, and he come home and said the hare told him he was wanted at home.

'Would you sell that hare?' says the fool of a man.

He said he would: he had the other hare handy in the cage and sure this *gaapey* of a man thought it was the one told her man to tell to come home. He bought the hare anyhow and went off.

That got him angered worse over the hare when he got home and found out.

'I'll get all my money back surely this day,' he says.

The man and the wife knew he'd be back and she was uneasy. Her man told her not to worry that he had a plan. And he put it to her. He killed a pig and caught the blood and got the bladder and filled it with the blood; and when he seen this fool of a man coming he run the bladder up in under his own woman's blouse or skirt or somewhere, and he got a knife. They started to argue - to blindfold the thing [pretend they were quarrelling] - and they fought out and into the street [yard] and when the fool of a man come near enough this man took the knife and he stuck his wife with the knife where the bladder was and she fell down and her all covered with blood.

'Jasus, you kilt her,' says the fool of a man.

'Ah sure,' says this other man, 'I do that on her every day. It puts manners on her. Only for that I couldn't live with her.'

And he takes out this horn and bent down and blew it in her ear. She let on to open her eyes and made some shape to rise.

'Aw John,' she says, 'you have me in a faint.'

And she got up as good as gold and went into the house.

'That's a great horn,' says the fool of a man. 'Would you sell it?'

Sells him the horn.

'For I have a divil of a woman at home,' says he.

So he goes home, and he sticks the wife with a knife, and he puts the horn to her ear and starts to blow. But sure if he was blowing till yet she wouldn't come to. That made him angrier than ever and he come at once and he caught the other man and seized him and put him in a bag and said he would drown him.

The tide was hitting up near the county road at Fathom. And the fool of a man fired him into the water and where hell did he light in the bag only on the root of an old thorn bush and that kept the bag [sack] up. So he started to sing. There was a man coming along the road driving a herd of cattle and he heard him singing and wondered what the hell he had to sing about in the bag. He wanted to know why he was singing.

'I'm going to Heaven,' says he.

'Heaven begod? I always wanted to go to Heaven. I'd like to go there.'

So they exchanged places and when he got this other boy in the bag he put a big lump of a stone in along with him and heaved him out. So he comes back himself driving the other fellow's herd of cattle. The fool of a man was all surprised to see him back – he thought he was dead, drownded - and he couldn't get over [understand reason of] the herd of cattle.

'Where'd you fall in with them?' says he.

'Where you threw me,' says this man.

'Down below?'

'The very place.'

'Would there be any more down there?'

'The only thing I regret,' says this man, 'is that I didn't have a servant-boy with me and I could have three times as many.'

So what hell then nothing would do him but he be to be put in a bag himself till he'd get some cattle. And when they come to the water this man says to the fool of a man:

'There's about the spot you threw me in.'

And here wasn't there all this blub-blub-blubbering coming from the fellow that had the cattle, in the bag below the water.

'What ails him?' says the fool of a man.

'It's the cattle. He can't count the cattle.'

He'd told him about this other fellow. So into the bag he went and was tied up and in he went and that was the last of the fool of a man too.

37a. The Blacksmith and the Tailor

Tailors they say will never see the Light of Heaven: something to do with the Divil. But the blacksmith's all right: he refused to make the nails to crucify Christ and the tinsmith made them and has a wandering foot ever since.

They used to say there was a tailor in Currainalt named Thady and he went to heaven. And this blacksmith went too and when he seen Thady he says to St Patrick and St Peter:

'I always thought no tailor would get into heaven?'

'Now,' says St Patrick, 'doesn't the world and its mother know Thady was never no tailor.'

He was only a botch ...!

37b

But this blacksmith and the tailor were courting this girl and maybe she had a bit of money or something; I don't know. Anyway the girl was for having the blacksmith and she told the tailor what she had in mind and he said she was foolish.

'Why am I foolish?' says she.

'You're going to marry a half-blind man.'

She asked how did he make that out, and the tailor told her to go to the forge and watch the blacksmith at work. And for every blow he'd hit the iron he'd miss six and hit the anvil: the way a blacksmith times his work. Good enough she went to the forge and I suppose the blacksmith put on a bit of a show seeing she was there and fairly timed his work, and she swore he was blind and wouldn't have him.

So the blacksmith asked her what put that in her head and she said the tailor had told her.

'In that case,' says the blacksmith, 'you're a bigger fool than ever. For he can't see at all.'

So she went to the tailor's shop to where he was working and sure you know what a tailor does when he wants to find the scissors under the cloth: he slaps the board he's sitting on and hears the scissors hop and gropes for them. When she saw that she run back like hell to the blacksmith and said he was right and that she'd have him!

38. A Wind-Broken Woman

There was this woman and she was a helluva powerful spinner of wool; and she had one daughter and the daughter was notoriously good-looking. But the daughter couldn't spin at all. So the trouble was how was she to get her off her hands.

Anyway this young lord bought a place in that part of the country and he got his eye on this woman's daughter and fell in love with her right away and before he could find out anything about her the pair were married. The mother of course said the girl was every bit as good a spinner as she was herself and the girl wondered and worried what would happen when the young lord found out.

'Leave all to me,' says the mother.

He married the girl and left in this hellishin great pile of wool for her to spin. He was going away on some business and said he expected to see it all spun by the time he got back. So away he went. The mother come of course and spun all the wool and had it all completed by the time the young lord got back.

Well, the young lord was highly delighted with the way the girl had spun the wool; he was that delighted he said he'd give a banquet, a great do in the castle. So he got everything ready and invited half the country.

And what did this old mother do? - Oh, a proper faggot in a way. She got a pig's bladder, and when she was going in to the banquet she blew it up and put it under her skirt somewhere. While they were eating and drinking every so often she'd give the bladder a squeeze and it would fart: till in the latter end the young lord took her outside and asked her what was wrong.

'I'm wind-broken,' says she, 'and that's from all the spinning I done in my time, and I suppose my girl will get wind-broken too if she doesn't give it up.'

So he made her quit - Told her to quit it: her that couldn't spin at all!

39. 'Had Your Agent Horns?'

It was this woman, a widow woman and she had one son that she was very fond of, but he was innocent [a simpleton]. There was a mill close by and this day she sent the son for some seeds to the mill or oatenmeal for to make something to ate. Things weren't so good with them and they were ready to be put out for want of paying the rent.

While the son was at the mill the mother was pounding spuds or washing clothes with a big wooden beetle and didn't the agent call for the rent, and whatever he said to her, or what he done, before she knew she up with the beetle and let him have it and stretches him full stretch on the floor. Killed him as dead as a door nail.

The job then was to get shut of him before the innocent son came back for she knew he'd tell the country and think no harm in it. And begod doesn't the boy come back and sees the agent.

'Did you kill him?' says he.

She kept the agent in the house till night and between them they carried the agent to the bog and dumps him in a bog-hole and they come home and go to bed. But when she gets the son asleep the mother gets up and back like hell down to the bog and whips the agent out.

She had an old buck-goat about the house and it had died and they'd buried it and she dug it up and dumps it in the bog-hole when she'd lugged the agent's body out, and she buried the agent where the buck-goat had been.

Well, the agent was missed and the poliss were out inquiring and searching everywhere, and sure they found out that the last place he was in was this widow woman's house and she said he had but had left, and doesn't the innocent boy let the cat out of the bag. They knew he was innocent but the poliss made him come and show him the bog-hole where he said him and the mother had thrown the body of the agent in.

So the boy jumps into the hole and feels the thing under his feet.

'Is he there?' says the polissman.

'Had your agent horns?' says he.

So they seen the buck-goat and that done it. They said they'd take no heed of the boy that he wasn't all in it and they went away.

40. The Man Who Lost An Eye

It was this man and he was at sea and he fell off the boat into the water and they threw a rope with a hook on the end of it to him to save him from drowning, and the hook struck him in the eye and he lost the eye. But he was saved.

Anyway when he landed on dry land he took law of them for the loss of his eye, and the case went on and was put back, went on and was put back I don't know how many times; because neither judge nor jury could see a way to settle it. All the lawyers and judges were bet and it was the talk of the whole country, on everyone's lips.

This lawyer was on the case anyhow and he could see no

way out of it all. He was walking along the road this evening, thinking hard. And here wasn't there two wee lads and they were trying the case too: everyone you understand was talking of it. So the lawyer stopped to listen to them.

'I could settle the case,' says one of the wee fellows.

'Could you?' says the other, and the lawyer standing listening to them; they didn't see him of course.

'I could settle it easy,' says this wee codger.

'How?' says the other fellow.

'I'd take this man out again in the boat,' says he, 'out in the boat to the self same place and throw him out in the sea; and then if he wanted to lose the other eye or drown they'd soon know.'

'I have him now,' says the lawyer and turns and walks home.

And that was the way the case was decided.

41. Unity is Strength

This old man was dying and he knew he was dying and he had three sons. So he called them to his bedside and he says to the eldest son for him to go out and bring him in a rush - a common rush. And he says to the second son:

'You go out and take me in another rush.'

And to the third son he said the same, and asked that a fourth rush be brought in for himself. The rushes were brought to him where he lay in the bed. He handed one to the eldest son and says he:

'Break that.'

Sure the eldest son took the rush in his hands and broke it, no bother in breaking a rush, catching it at the two ends, and pulling.

'You all see that,' says the old man.

They said they did.

'Now,' says he, 'let yous all go till I call yous.'

They left him to himself and he took the three remaining rushes and he plaited them and when he had that done he called them up again to his bedside. He handed the plaited rushes to the eldest son.

'Break that,' says he.

Well, if he was pulling till yet he couldn't break the plaited rushes: or the second son couldn't break it: nor the youngest son when it come his turn.

'Now then,' says the father, 'that's the way you'll be when I'm gone. If yous stay together yous can't be broken.'

42. Half a Blanket

This son was married and he had a young son himself in the cradle, and the old grandfather, the son's father was knocking about, not much good then for anything only eating and smoking. So the son of the old fellow said the old man would have to go; leave - that was the word: take the broad road for it.

Well, his own son, the child was in the cradle. And the wife was pleading with her husband for to give the old man a chance but he wouldn't listen. So she pleaded with her husband to give the old fellow a blanket when he was ready to go.

'Give him a whole blanket,' says she.

The son was for giving him half a blanket but he says: 'All right. I'll give a whole blanket.'

'Do no such'n a thing,' says the child in the cradle. 'Give him only half a blanket and keep the other half safely by. For I'll need it when I have to give it to you when it's my turn to put you out to the world.'

That was from the child that couldn't talk. So the old fellow was let stay, he wouldn't get leave then to go at all, when the son heard what his own child had in store for himself.

43. Father and Son

There was another son was for putting his father away when he was done and no good only for eating. So they argued about it but it come to the whipping of crutches and he was for away and the son was leaving the father a piece and seeing him off the place. They come to this big stone sticking out of the ditch.

'Let me sit on this stone awhile,' says the old man, 'for when I was leaving my father away he asked to sit a while on this stone.'

'You're far enough,' says the son. 'Come on back.'

44. 'You're a Liar!'

There was a wealthy big buck one time, a lord and he had a million of money and one daughter. And he said he'd give the daughter to any man if he could make him, the lord, call him a liar. The fellow coming looking the girl would have to set out to tell a story and make him call him a liar back.

Anyway this fellow on the road heard of it and thought he might as well try his luck: though I think you lost your head if you failed. He goes in and he started off:

'There was seven sows one time and they had seven litters in this big spud ...'

'Man a man,' says the lord, 'do you tell me that?'

'And there was seven horses and seven carts carting pig-dung out of this big spud for seven weeks ...'

'I well believe you,' says the lord.

'And there was seven women cutting seed-priddies for seven weeks off the same big priddy ...'

'I well believe you.'

'And coming away I met a fox and I hit him seven kicks in the arse and he let three farts and any one of them was cleaner nor you ...'

'You're a liar!' says the lord.

So he got the woman.

45. 'Brigid Bucked Him'

He was an old farmer and a miser living his lone only for the servant girl, Brigid, and she'd been a lifetime with him. He was always saying she'd get his money; that was for to stay on with him and look after him. Anyway he took very bad this day and he knew he'd come to die. So he called Brigid to his bedside and says he to her:

'Do you see that chest there, Brigid?'

She sayed she did.

'Open it,' says he, 'and take out a bowl and bring it to me here to the bed.'

She done what she was bid and took out this bowl, and it was full to the brim of gold sovereigns.

'Now,' says he to Brigid, 'go down to the kitchen and take up the best saucepan you have to me here.'

So she took up the saucepan and he told her what to do.

'Empty them into the saucepan,' he says, 'and then put them on the fire till they're melted. Then come and tell me.'

Brigid took the saucepan of sovereigns down to the kitchen and was about to do as she was bid when she says to herself:

'Why should I do that ...?'

And what hell does she do? She empties out the sovereigns and puts in a good lump of butter instead and puts the saucepan on the fire. And didn't a few of the sovereigns happen to stick. He calls down from the room, for he wasn't fit to rise any more:

'Are they not melted yet?'

'In a wee while,' she says; 'any minute now.'

'Take it up the minute it's melted. And take a cup with you as well,' says he.

So when all the butter was melted she put in these few sovereigns in the bottom, gets the cup, and takes all up to him in the bed. He took the cup and scalding hot mind you ... let all down.

'There's one or two,' says Brigid, 'in the bottom that didn't get time to melt.'

'Then take them back and give them another wee heat,' says he.

So she let on to do that and melted more butter. He was a miser and he thought to drink all the money he had so she'd get none of it. But Brigid bucked him!

46. Whang the Miller Makes a Match

He was a fellow called Whang the Miller; why I don't know; and he went with this fellow to a house to make a match and there was three nice girls in it; they were going to get a match made. They decided they'd stop for the night, and the woman of the house she made a big pot of colcannon - they call it 'bruisey' now - and she put plates out in front of them do you see.

'Now,' says Whang the Miller to the other fellow before they went in, 'don't disgrace yourself; don't ate too much.'

'How will I know when I'm to stop?'

'I'll stand on your foot.'

There was an ould dog, do you see, and he was under the table and he lay down on the fellow's foot - and he just quit eating all of a sudden.

'Is that all you can ate? Aw, well, you have a bad appetite,' says the woman of the house.

'Aw,' he says, 'a very poor appetite.'

But sure Whang the Miller finished his plate.

Wèll, they went off up to bed: they went to bed anyway.

'Jasus,' he says, 'and do you know - I'm mad with the bleddy hunger. What did you put your toe on me foot for? Sure I'd have liked to ate more.'

'I didn't.'

'Well, some bleddy thing bruised me foot to the ground sure.'

'It was the ould dog under the table,' says Whang the Miller, 'that lay on you. I didn't touch you. Didn't touch you at all.'

'Christ Jasus,' he says, 'I'm mad with hunger.'

Whang the Miller says: 'There's a big welter of colcannon below in the kitchen on the side dish on the table.'

'Be Christ I'll go down for another feed of yon. It was grand stuff. But Jasus,' he says, 'how will I know the room when I come back?'

'Well, here,' says Whang the Miller; 'follow this spool of thread; catch that and go on down. Tie it to the leg of the table, or tie it to a chair and,' he says, 'follow that back up again.'

He did. So when Whang the Miller got the boyo down didn't he bring over the spool and thread and didn't he throw it in - Opened the door and threw it in where the lassie was: one big lump of a lassie, lying there. He come up, and he come up, and Whang the Miller told him to take some of the colcannon up to him. He went in in the dark and he says:

'Here's a bit for you.'

He lifted the clothes and he just clapped it to her end in the dark. And he got in to bed. Slept anyway.

Next morning her ladyship was up and she calls the boys. Went into the room: there was only one fellow Whang the Miller in the room do you see. She went into the other room, and she seen the plate and she seen everything; and she just lifted the clothes - the two of them was dead asleep:

'Aw, Jasus, he must have give Mary a shocking revvin'; he put the colcannon out behind her. We better get them married at once.'

47. The Fool Who Escaped From Hell

Two men crossing to England to sell a drove of goats were short-handed and took along a fool to help them. But in England the fool was so over-awed with the sights that he was more a hindrance than a help.

So they bought a bottle of whiskey - it was cheap then - set him drunk and left him lying at the pit-head of a coal-mine, intending to pick him up later after they had sold the goats.

Miners going to work saw the fool, put him in a cage, and took him down the mine. When he awoke out of his drunken slumber he was in almost pitch darkness, could hear distant rumblings and could see low tunnels running in all directions. Then a man as black as the Earl of Hell's waistcoat appeared with a light in his forehead - the miner with his lamp.

'Where am I?' whispered the fool.

'Where do you expect?' says the miner back to him: 'you died in drink and you're in Hell. Are you hungry?'

The fool said he was: the miner gave him some of his own 'piece' [lunch]. He ate that.

'Do you want a smoke?' says the miner.

The fool said he did: the miner gave him his own [the fool's] plug and he had a smoke. Then the miner asks:

'Are you dry?'

The fool said he was: and the miner handed him his own bottle of whiskey the drover's had bought.

'Put that to your head and finish it,' the miner ordered.

He lowered it all and fell back drunk once more.

His companions returned, found him missing, and crossed back to Ireland, believing he had gone before them. Coming off work the miners took the fool up in the cage and left him lying where they had found him at the pit-head.

When the fool awoke and found daylight he hurried to the boat and crossed back to Ireland. It was Sunday and he walked to his home parish, and was just in time to go to Mass. When he went into the chapel the priest was preaching on tortures of Hell, and he cried:

'And out of Hell there is no redemption.'

The fool stood up and called back to the priest: 'You're far enough with that crack, Father. It's no later than yesterday I was in Hell and I was never better treated in my life.'

48. A Mighty Pick

Two Irishmen crossed to England to look for work as navvies.

At the dockside they separated, each promising to return to the spot that evening to tell how they had got on.

When one man returned he found the other sitting on a bollard staring at a rusted old ship's anchor lying agin a wall.

'What are you doing?' asked the other.

'I'm waiting to see the man who is going to use that pick,' says he.

49. The Lazy Daughter

It was this old gentleman farmer and he had three daughters. Two were good working girls, but the third one would do nothing; everything had to be done for her. So the father said he would give a hundred pounds to anyone that'd marry either of the other two; and two hundred pounds ... Two hundred mark you! ... to anyone that'd marry the lazy one.

He had a damned good reason for that. He was always under the opinion that no one would take the lazy one, and unless he give more money to her than the others she hadn't a chance. He never thought to get rid of her.

But this fellow anyway was down in money and he said to himself that if he took this one with the two hundred of money he'd be right again. So he come looking [for] her.

He took her and they got married, and there was a month's visit that time: the bride wouldn't go home to her parents' place until a month would be up, but before the month was up the man meant to go.

There was a servant boy and girl in the place and the day before they were to go the boy and girl got ham and eggs, and she took it to them.

'What's the reason,' says she to him, that they get ham and eggs and I don't?'

'They work,' says he.

'In that case,' says she, 'we'll do a little.'

So begod she started working to do a little.

The time had come to make the visit, but before the month was up, and he had an old rusty horse [refuse to work or haul loads if the notion took hold]; it would always rust in the trap or the cart at the foot of this hill.

So they set off in the trap for the father's place, and at the foot of this hill the old horse rusted, and he says to this woman:

'Get down out of the trap.'

She got out of the trap and he had a pistol and he went up and he shot the horse stone dead.

'Get him loosed out,' says he to the wife.

So she loosed the draught chains and pulled the old horse by the tail to the side of the road ... he was standing by there all the time not rising his hand [to help her] and then he says:

'Now, you get into the shafts.'

So she pulled and he driv her into the yard and the servants run up to help her. By the time they got there the other two son-in-laws had arrived with their women and were already waiting. The others were up in the room playing cards and the minute he went in with his woman the father told her to join the others in the room playing the cards. So she did. The old gentleman then says:

'I'm giving fifty pounds to whichever one of yous has the most biddable woman.'

'My woman,' says the fellow married to the eldest girl, 'is the most biddable woman.'

The second said the same and the fellow with the lazy woman said that his woman couldn't be bet. So the old father said he'd put it to the test and in turn they were to call the girls from the room. The eldest fellow started first and he says:

'You're a-wanting up here,' says he.

'I'll be up now,' says she; 'I only want a five of the game.'

So when she come up he says to her:

'That's all right: you can go back now.'

So the second fellow was next and he called his woman.

'I'm dealing the cards,' she says; 'I'll be up in a minute.'

She come up and was sent back, and then it was the third fellow's turn to call the lazy one.

'Come up here,' he says to her.

'Yes,' she says, 'I will be with you now. Immediately!'

He got the fifty pounds. He had the life scared out of her, and she was a good working woman ever after.

That's the story as well as I can remember it; I can't tell it right now or think of the half of it, but you have the most of it anyway.

'Who told it to me ...? Aw, God's truth if I could tell you now ... Maybe that man we were talking about a while ago, Murtey McGaley or one of the other old lads. Some one of them anyway. Sure Lord help you man it's years since I heard them cracks told.

50. The King Who Had to Cry 'Quit!'

It was this king in Ireland one time that offered his only daughter in marriage to anyone that could tell a story without an end: if he told a story that had an end he would be beheaded unless he could make the king tell him to stop.

So this fellow decided to try his luck and he started to tell this story:

'Once upon a time there was a man and he built a granary for himself, and he had seven times seven acres of oats. He filled the granary with oats till it was right full to the top, to the very roof.

'Then there came a plague of something like locusts to the country and they lit on the barn or the granary and found one wee hole on top, the roof, and it was that small it would let in only one of these locusts at a time.

'So one locust went in and took out a grain of the oats; and another locust went in and took out a grain of the oats and come out; and another locust went in and got a grain of the oats and come out; and another locust got up and went in and come out with a grain of the oats ...'

'Tell us what happened but?' cried the king.

'I can't tell you, sir,' says he, 'till they've got all the oats out. For there was millions of pickles of corn, and it was two or three years before they got them all out.

'So there was another locust went in and took out a pickle of oats ...'

'Quit it! Stop!' cries the king. 'Take my daughter.'

51a. He Came on the Lord's Daughter A-Drowning

It was this wee lad and he was gathering sticks at this gentleman's place; and he came on the lord's daughter a-drowning. But be the Holy Sailor anyway he couldn't reach her, and the rope he had for the sticks, he threw her the rope and she caught a-hold of the end of that and he managed to pull her to the bank.

Well, the lord, the gentleman, he sent for him, and for his father, and he said he would school and educate the wee lad, so that when he grew up he'd be fit [suitable spouse] to marry his daughter.

And he was as good as his word and the wee lad was schooled and educated and all the rest. But when it come to courting the girl he couldn't put his arm round her, and he was on the back of the book [in disfavour].

For she had a puzzle for him and said she would never marry him anyway, and she told him what he had to work out. Here it is: listen close now:

'For my breakfast you must get
A bird without a bone;
And for my dinner, a cherry without a stone;
And for my supper, a bird without a gall
Before I'd lie one night you
At either stock or wall.'

After hearing that he was in the Divil's way [confused] and he was going round talking to himself and could make no headway at all. But this old hag, an old witch of a woman, was going by and she heard him talking to himself, and she says:

'Aw, *avick*, [son] what's wrong with you?'

So he told her. And says she:

'Aw sure that's easy got; very easy,' says she.

And here's what she told him:

'When the bird is in the shell
it really has no bone;
When the cherry is in blossom
it really has no stone:
The dove she is a gentle bird
And flies without a gall,
So you and me in the one bed lie
And you lie next the wall.'

Well, he went to the girl with that, but she had more questions for him. Says she:

'Answer me three questions three
Before I'd lie one night with you
At either stock or wall:

What's deeper nor the sea?
What's higher nor a tree?
What's worse nor woman's work?
Before I'd lie one night with you
At either stock or wall.'

Well, he was in hell altogether with that and was going round talking away to himself, and here doesn't he come across the old lassie again, the hag, and she asked him what was wrong now and he told her his story. So she answered for him. Says she:

'Heaven's higher nor a tree:
Hell's deeper nor the sea:
The Divil's work is worse nor woman's work;
So you and me, in the one lie
And you lie next the wall.'

That's it. He got the girl. It was a song as well. I heard it and me only a wee lad myself.

6 TALES OF HISTORICAL FIGURES

The storytellers: Annie Lynch, left, with her daughter and son-in-law

52. Dan O'Connell and the Eldest Twin

It was these two brothers that got a big legacy from someone in Belfast and they lived outside the town here; a big pull of money. They were two twins and the money was left to the youngest son. Well, they fell out about the money and they lawed and lawed damn near to the last cow at the stake and it ended up in The Four Courts in Dublin and Dan O'Connell was called in.

O'Connell it seems had all this thrashed out before he took on the case at all and he was for the youngest twin. He said that the last of the twins to be born was the eldest, for, says O'Connell, he was the first to be conceived in the mother's womb.

The way O'Connell put it was: 'The first corn that went into the sack was the oldest.'

And that was that. The youngest brother of the twins got the legacy - or all that was left of it after the lawyers got their whack.

53. Dan O'Connell Meets His Match

The cleverest man in the world the day can meet his match and O'Connell met his one time, only it was a woman.

She stole a cow and was in bad trouble and when O'Connell come to the town on some law case she thought she might as well burn the candle when she'd burnt the inch and see him. So she did and explained her case to him. Maybe the cow was lifted off her for debt or something and she stole it back: she had some story like that anyway. O'Connell listened to her and he says:

'Your case is bad and you could get transported. But,' says he, 'if I get you off scot free can you pay me?'

'I can not,' says she.

'Well,' says he, 'what have you at home?'

'I have one good brave fat pig,' says the woman.

'If I win the case and get you free will you give me the pig then?'

'I will with pleasure,' she says.

He said that was all right, that would do, and told her where she was to drive the pig to some yard in the town for him. So she promised on all that was high and holy she would leave the pig for him if he won the case for her.

'Now,' says O'Connell, 'when you're taken out and stood in

the dock they'll ask you your name and they'll ask you this, that and the other. But no matter what they ask you you're not to make them any answer only the one: "Let you be eating scallions." When they ask you a question says you: "Would you ate a scallion?" '

She said she would and she was called and stood in the dock and the case began.

'What's your name?' says the clerk.

'Would you ate a scallion?' says she.

'Answer the question, mam,' says the judge.

'Would you ate a scallion?' says she to him.

'Do you hear what I said?' the judge asks.

'Would you ate a scallion?' says she again.

'Take her away,' says the judge. 'The woman's not half-right in the head. The case is dismissed.'

So she got free. And when she come out of the court there was Dan O'Connell and him all smiles.

'Now, my decent woman,' says he, 'let you go and get that pig and drive it into that yard.'

'Would you ate a scallion?' says she to Dan.

And that's all he could get out of her either.

54. Dan O'Connell: A Son of His Da's

Dan O'Connell was a going boy too in his day ... Truth or lies the story was told on him. He was fond of the weemen too. One day when he went back home to Kerry or Cork or wherever it was he lived he met this lad on the road. Dan was a big man at this time. He asked the lad his name and he told him and he asked him who his Da was and he said he had no father or the father was dead or something. So Dan asked him his mother's name and the lad told him, and Dan reached the lad a golden guinea.

'Next time I meet you,' says Dan, 'I'll give you another golden guinea.'

The lad walked on, but round the bend of the road he hopped the ditch and away like hell back the way he come, over the ditches, and round another bend hopped out on the road and met Dan again. Dan put his hand in his pocket and reached him the guinea.

'You're a son of your Da's all right,' says he.

55. Dan Teaches Ireland How to Whistle

Dan O'Connell was the first man in Ireland that learned an Irishman how to whistle with four fingers, two fingers of every hand in your mouth. He learned them that for a warning: so's they'd be able to give warning.

The same as the Night of the Straws. He put on a bet that he'd rise Ireland in twenty-four hours. So a straw be to be left in every house. I'd run with a straw to your house and you be to run with it to another and everyone in the house be to run until there wasn't a house in all Ireland hadn't a straw and they were all standing ready.

56. Dan Told Him to Sow Peas

An Irishman emigrating to America was penniless. Before boarding the ship he asked a woman to cook him a meal and promised to pay for it when he would return. She did so and fried him two eggs.

When he returned after a number of years he went to pay the woman. She demanded a huge sum of money, and explained that had she hatched the two eggs they would have produced two chickens which would in turn lay and these eggs could be hatched, and so on.

The man went to O'Connell. Dan said he would have to 'stand the court' and directed him to fill his pockets with dried peas; and when called to testify to 'sow' the peas around the floor of the courthouse.

The man did as Dan directed. When asked by the judge what he was doing, Dan replied that the peas had as much chance of growing on the boarded floor of the courthouse as two fried eggs had of hatching out of two chickens.

57. Redmond O'Hanlon and the Servant Boy

Many a time Redmond O'Hanlon held up a coach on the road over at Edenappa and the Gap of the North and only himself in it, and it'd be guarded with soldiers. He'd have heads of cabbage in the hedge and hats on them and let on they were his men. But a wee servant boy in Dundalk tricked him.

This lad was hired with a big Dundalk merchant and the merchant had to collect a debt in gold in Newry, but he was afeared of O'Hanlon robbing him. No one would face to go for fear of Redmond. And the wee servant boy said he would go.

'Good man,' says the merchant, 'and I'll get you the fastest horse in the stable.'

'I don't want the fastest horse,' says the wee codger, 'but give me the worse old horse you can lay your hands on. And I'll want no pistol.'

Well, they couldn't understand why he wanted an old done slow horse and he wouldn't tell them. But he guaranteed the merchant that he'd have the gold back with him safe and sound.

'I'll see and make it worth your while,' says the merchant. 'It's a bargain.'

Off the wee codger sets sail on the old horse. And of course somewhere half-way he meets this fine looking gentleman, well dressed and riding a very fine horse.

'Good day, me boy,' says the gentleman.

'Good day, sir,' says the boy.

'Where are you going?' asks the gentleman.

'I'm going as far as Newry,' says the boy, 'to lift a debt in gold for my master but I'm heart afeared of meeting Redmond O'Hanlon.'

'Don't be one bit afeared,' says the gentleman. 'I'll be here when you're coming back and I'll see you come to no harm.'

And of course who hell was it only Redmond O'Hanlon himself.

Well, the boy rode on and one way and another reached Newry and got the debt in gold in a wee sack or satchel. But he changed one of the sovereigns and said he wanted it all in small coppers. Ties it. He puts the satchel of sovereigns in-inunder the saddle and hangs the sack of coppers on the saddle. Mounts up and away back for Dundalk.

Well, when he come to the place - there was a wood there along the road - here he meets the same gentleman sitting waiting on his fine horse.

'Well,' says he, 'did you do your job?'

'I did,' says the boy.

'And where's the gold?'

'I have it here with me,' says the boy.

'Then,' says Redmond, 'your money or your life. I'm Redmond O'Hanlon. Hand it over.'

'Well,' says the boy, 'I never believed in handing money to anyone in my life. Go and pick it up.'

And he whipped the bag of coppers off the saddle and fires it well into the wood. Redmond laughed and got down off his fine horse and away into the wood to get the sack, and then off with the servant off his old horse, leaps on Redmond's fine horse, and away galloping like mad for Dundalk. And of course Redmond hadn't a hope in hell of overtaking and catching him on the old horse.

58. Redmond's Proof of Shot Shirt

Redmond O'Hanlon could only be shot with his own gun for he wore a Proof of Shot Shirt and no bullets from another gun would go through it. It was a shirt made of flax, a linen shirt: the flax had to be pulled after sunrise and dry-hackled and scutched and spun and woven and made up all before the same day's sun went down, and that made a Proof of Shot Shirt.

Sure the day he was shot at Eight Mile Bridge here below Hilltown it was Hilltown Fair, and when the sound of the shot sounded some of them run for they knew the sound of Redmond's gun. His foster-brother Art lifted Redmond's gun and shot him for the reward and a pardon when he got him asleep in the hut: though you'd gct ones to tell you it was a jealous girl of his own country working here round Hilltown shot him, and that then Art seen it was no good to try to save him.

59a. Dean Swift Finds a Clever Boy

Did you ever hear a story of the Dean Swift? Laurence Woods here [a man from the Hilltown district of County Down] has all them cracks, an' about Dan O'Connell, but he's as deaf as a hatchet.

The Dean was advertisin' for a boy, an' he was to be neither ridin' nor walkin', barefooted or shod. Neither ridin' nor walkin', nor barefooted nor shod, an' he was to answer all that was put till him [questions].

So anyway on the day appointed they all gathered at the

Dean's Castle, an' there was a lawn to it, a big lawn, don't you see? So the Dean was there an' he was askin' them what they could do, an' what they couldn't do, an' they were to be neither ridin' nor walkin' nor barefooted nor shod.

So this boy was there in answer to the advertisement of the Dean. So they [the other applicants] were there an' they couldn't make it; and so begod he got a sow pig an' he took her down the lawn, an' he got a boot off an' he threw it over the ditch. So here he throws one leg over the sow an' he come up the lawn. That was neither ridin' nor walkin', an' he wasn't neither barefooted nor shod, don't you see.

So the Dean was standin' watchin' an' he thought him very clever. So the Dean says till him says he:

'What are you goin' to do?' he says to the boy.

'Nothin',' says he.

So begod the Dean looks at him an' says he:

'An' what took you here?' says he.

'Well,' says the boy back, 'I'm listenin' to all them goin' to do everythin'. So when they do all I have nothin' to do,' says he.

So anyway the Dean kept him.

The Dean had a coach, an' he was to drive the coach as well for the Dean. So he had to rize early, an' begod this mornin' he slept in, an' do you see he had no time to take his breakfast. So they were drivin' in the coach, an' the Dean was prayin' ... he be to be a Protestant, the Dean. So begod anyway he was prayin' in the coach. But anyway they went down the road an' they met a man, an' the man stopped to ask them where they were goin'.

'We're goin' to Heaven,' says the boy.

So the man says:

'How do you make that appear that you're goin' to Heaven?' says he.

'Well,' says the boy, 'he's prayin' an' I'm fastin'.' [the Roman Catholic edict requiring believers to fast penitentially at stated periods] ' ... Wasn't that a good one?

So they went on an' into a house, an' the Dean was very angry. I think the boy left him an' went home.

So do you see wasn't he sittin' he's lone when the Dean come for him to go back.

'Are you sittin' your lone?' says he.

'I am,' says the boy.

'An' none but yourself,' says the Dean. 'An' where's your father?' says the Dean.

'He's pullin' down ditches [fences] to build gaps,' says the boy.

'An' where's your mother?' says the Dean.

'She's out fowlin',' says the boy, 'an' what she doesn't catch an' kill she'll bring an' take in.'

'That's a queer job,' says the Dean. 'An' where's your sister?' says he.

'She's cryin' for the pony she had last year,' says the boy.

So the Dean stood awhile and says he:

'That's a very queer job,' says he. 'What do you mean your father's out pullin' down ditches to build gaps?'

'Well,' says the boy, 'he's away out to *brerd* whins [gorse: to cut for fencing]. He's cuttin' down the whins to build up gaps.'

An' that was like it: wasn't that pullin' down ditches to build up gaps don't you see?

'An' what do you mean your mother's out fowlin' an' what she'll catch an' kill she won't take in?'

'Well,' says the boy, 'she took a notion that there was a flea in the blanket,' says he, 'an' so all she'll see she'll catch an' kill an' all she's doesn't she'll take in.' [Delousing.]

'An' what do you mean your sister's cryin' for the pony she had last year?' says the Dean.

'Well,' says the boy, 'she happened to have a mistake with a young fellow last year [had an illegitimate child] an' she's away cryin' about it.'

So anyway he went back to the Dean. An' he went on along. I think the Dean must have been a Protestant, for they were drivin' to church. So when they come to the church it was wrote above the door:

'No admission to Roman Catholics.'

So the boy wrote under it:

'Whoever wrote this they wrote it well,
For the same is on The Gates of Hell?'

Did you ever hear that afore?

59b.

The Dean orders the boy to cook a goose for dinner. Being hungry the boy eats a leg of the goose: when served the Dean asks why there aren't two legs. It was a cold day and the boy invited the Dean to look at the geese standing outside - on one leg. The Dean walks over and says:

'Whoosh.' The geese run away on two legs.

The boy says:

'Why didn't you say "whoosh" to your dinner?'

60a. Dean Swift Meets a Lawyer's Funeral

Dean Swift and his boy are held up by the funeral of a lawyer; the coffin is being carried by colleagues of the dead man. In reply to a query from the boy the Dean says:

'One rogue over and four under,
The body's going to the grave
The soul's going a journey:
The Divil's at law and wants an attorney.'

60b.

Attributed to Dean Swift about a town which need not be named:

'In ...... town
Without renown,
With church, tower and steeple;
In every door
There stands a whore
Looking at decent people.'

7

WANDERERS AND TRAMPS

The storytellers: Tom Dunne, left, and Mick Murphy ('Mick Dinning'), third from left

61. The Fenian Secrets

James O'Kane of Coleraine told this to my mother one night and I heard him: it's his story.

He was on banishment for making poteen and he took all the back roads and by-roads and let on he was looking for work until he come into Donegal. He was on this by-road and it came on a bad night blowing and raining and storming. And away a bit in the distance he seen this light. So he made for that. He come to this lane from the road up to this house and turns in and didn't get far up the lane when he met a man coming down.

'Where are you for?' says the man till him.

'I'm looking for work and a night's shelter,' says James. And at the same time he had sovereigns galore in his pocket, maybe a hundred.

The man says: 'I have to go to my master to sit up with a cow that's bad. Tell my wife,' says the man. 'That's my house and we're not long married: tell my wife you met me and she'll let you in.'

He went to the house and he rapped on the door.

'Who's that?' says she. 'Is it you back?'

'It is not,' says James, 'but I'm looking for work and a night's shelter and I met your husband and he said for you to let me in.'

'Get away,' says she.

'I'm a stranger,' says James; 'your husband said for you to let me in.'

'I dare him!' says she. 'I dare him to send a strange man to come in to me.'

Well, he turned away. But away to the north-east of the house he saw this thing: he thought it was a room till he looked but he could see no door: so he climbed up on the end and made a hole and come down damn near on top of her and he could see the kitchen and a great fire burning in the grate and all and he could feel the heat of it. On that side there was a bed, that side a table. Next thing he hears a foot coming to the door and says he:

'If this is the husband back again I'll get in now.'

Well, she opened the door and this man come in and it wasna her husband and he threw his arms round her and give her two or three hugs and went up to the fire and sat down and pulled out half-a-pint of whiskey and reached it till her. She went down to the dresser and took out a cake and put it and the whiskey on the table. She sat down a while with him at the fire and they ate some of the cake and had a drink of whiskey - James was watching it all. Then she got up and lifted a bowl on the dresser and took out a cooked hen and they sat down and joined to ate the hen and the cake and drink the whiskey.

There was a bing of straw at the low end of the kitchen. After a while he knowed it wasn't her own man - this man had on a sleeve-waistcoat and he knew it wasn't her husband. The next thing James hears was another foot, and the man and the wife made a splutter and he got under the straw in the corner and hid himself. She run and put the hen back under the bowl and put the whiskey aback of the plates on the dresser: James said he knowed that whiskey bottle - it was more like a sucking-bottle he sayed. And she hid the cake somewhere else. Her own man rapped the door.

'Open the door or I'll break it down,' he says.

She opened the door and she joined to cry.

'Sending a strange man to me,' she says and let on she thought it was the strange man back again for why she delayed in opening the door.

'You have a brave good fire on,' says the husband.

'Ock, sure,' she says, 'I never got to bed. I was that feert I meant to sit up till you would come.'

'The man wouldna touch you,' says he.

So when James heard that he crawled out the way he got in and come round to the door and rapped it to be let in.

'Who's there?' says the wife.

'The man you wouldn't let in,' says James.

So he was let in. The husband says to him:

'What part are you from?'

'Armagh,' says James.

'You're all Fenians up there,' says the husband. 'So before you get a bite to ate or a place to lie down you'll tell me the Fenian secrets.'

'I give it all up years ago,' says James.

'You'll get your fill of oaten-bread and tea,' says the husband, 'when you tell me. Three words will do or you won't stay here.'

'It's very hard,' says James. 'But if I have to do it I suppose I must.' And he says: 'Have you a riddle.' So the husband got him a riddle he had for cleaning the oats. 'Give it to me,' says James. 'Now, have you a wee grain of oats?' He put the corn in the riddle and went over some gibberish or gubbish.

'Is that the Irish of it?' says the husband.

James sayed that it was.

'Give it to me then in English,' says the husband.

'It wouldn't do,' says James, 'if I give it in English.' And says he then after more gibberish: 'Will you lift thon bowl on the dresser.'

The husband lifted the bowl.

'Holy Jasus,' says he, 'a hen with only a leg off her.'

'Put him out,' shouts the wife, 'he's the Divil. He has the Black Art,' she joined to shout.

Again James went over some gibberish and he says:

'Lift thon second plate on the dresser.'

And the wife reached for something and said she would knock his brains out that he be to be the Divil.

The husband got the whiskey behind the plate.

'That's all now,' says James Kane.

'You promised three words,' says the husband, 'or out you go.'

'It's a very hard task,' says James. So he goes down and opens the door and says more gibberish and says he:

'Have you a flail?'

'I have.'

'Will you give me the flail?' says he. He got the flail in his hands. And he handed the flail to the husband and showed him the bing of straw in the corner. 'When I tell you to thrash you start to thrash,' says he, 'and that's the lot. The finish.'

The husband took the flail and swung it and started to thrash, and the man hiding under the straw run out and the husband winded the flail to hit him and then the wife. It was the husband's master was under the straw. She was a servant with him before he got the husband to take for some reason or other. He hit the wife and says she:

'You'll never heat sheet or blanket with me again,' she says till her husband and he put her out and away she goes. So when she was gone James got something to ate and they ate the cake and the hen and drunk the whiskey and the husband give him a few shillings as well, but James never let on he had sovereigns in his pocket and he got staying till morning.

62. The Three Advices

There was a man one time lived away up somewhere by the mountain by Knockbarra, and he got married, and very soon after he got married he left and went away on a boat from Warrenpoint or somewhere to work in England. Year after year he worked in England and never come home, working all the time with this same farmer. So this day he says to himself that he should think of going home: he'd left the wife at home and never once seen her from the day he left or wrote or a God's cursed haet. So this day he says to the English farmer he was working with:

'I'm in a notion of going home.'

'When?' says the farmer.

'Soon,' says he.

So he told him: he told the farmer he had a woman at home in Ireland - The farmer didn't know till then that he was married. He was going home anyway.

So when the farmer seen he was for going he says till him:

'Well, you're a good while here and you never lifted no money or wages. What'll you take?' says the farmer. 'Will you take it all an' nothin' else; or will you take some of it, a loaf and three advices?'

Well, this fellow sayed the advices would be good, but the advice wouldn't be much good without the money, so he'd take a little of the money and the three advices.

'Right,' says the farmer. 'One advice I'm going to give you: Never go a near-cut while you have the hard, level road going round.'

And he says:

'Another advice I'll give you: Never stay where an old man is married to a young woman. A third advice I'll give you: never do in your passion what you might rue after.'

Them was the three advices he give him. And then the farmer says till him:

'My wife is baking the loaf of bread for you to take on your journey. And my advice to you would be not to break on it if you can till you get near home.'

So he took the loaf and steered for home. He come anyway to this house and it was getting late and he thought he might as well look for lodgings there for the night. He got the lodgings and something to ate. And there was this young woman and this old fellow in the house and he took her to be the old fellow's daughter. So when she had all redd up about the house ... she out and away and left the house to them.

The old fellow in the house was a kind of dull on it for a while; and then he started to talk about the young woman and the way she was always running out of the house on him especially at night and he didn't know what in hell to do.

'Why,' says the man that was making his road home, 'is she your wife?'

The old man said she was and this fellow when he heard that thought of the advice given to him and says: 'Then I'm long enough here.'

He slipped out on the old fellow, but he didn't keep to the road: there was a meadow with hay in it near the house and he seen this stack in it and he says: 'I'll make meself comfortable here in this stack till morning.'

He got rooted into the stack and dozed off, and in a while he heard these voices; some woman talking to a man one side of the stack. And she was saying:

'There's a travelling man staying the night in our house,' she says, 'and he's bound to have money. We'll kill him the night and throw his body near the cut road.'

Well, the heart trimbled in him when he heard that: it was the old fellow's wife and she had this man on her string and they wanted money. Anyway, he kept still till they went away and when they left he got out of the stack and away for his life.

On he come: got as far as the boat and took the boat and got home. He lived as I told you away up on the mountain near Knockbarra, in a wee house stuck in-inunder this rock on the mountain. The door was spriced up - there was a spade or something inside to the back of it to keep it up and keep it closed at the same time.

He put his shoulder to the door anyway and made in. His wife that he hadn't seen for God knows how long since the day or so after he married her was lying on some kind of a shake-down of a bed in the corner, and there was this man lying with her.

This man that was lying with the wife put his head up above the blankets when she started to shout: 'Who was there?' and 'What's was up?' and he seen this face of beard on the man lying with her: a great black beard. And when he seen this man with the beard in bed with his own wife he run back to the door to get the spade holding up the door and he lifted it and turned and was going to make two divides of the man in bed with his wife. And she shouts:

'Are you going to kill your own son?'

The woman had a son to him and he didn't know ... Didn't know his own son till she told him. So she got up anyway and lit the fire and they got some light. And he give her the loaf to make something to ate for the three of them. And when she went to cut it there was a purse of gold in it; in the heart of the loaf.

63. The Gallows Thief

There was this man one time and he had a big lump of a codger of a son and he was fit for nothing only thievery: Oh, a gallows thief. So he allowed that the only thing for him was to take the codger and apprentice him to an old Master Thief and let him learn the trade right. So he done that.

The Old Thief said he didn't know whether he could take the codger on or not.

'You may,' says the father, 'for if he stays around our place he'll never be out of trouble.'

'If he's not fit to do the tasks I lay out for him,' says the Old Thief, 'he'll lose his head or I'll shoot him for he'd know as much as myself.'

'Fair enough,' says the father, 'for he'll only be hung one day anyhow if he goes on the way he's going.'

So the Old Thief took this codger on to train him. And the first task he give him was that night he was to steal the sheet from the bed from inunder this man and his wife, and the man would know he was coming to steal the sheet, and if he got his lamps on him he would shoot him dead.

'Fair enough,' says the codger.

Night come and he goes to this graveyard and he digs up

this corpse that was only buried and he lapped it in a grass-seed bag [sack] and goes to this gentleman's house and gets a ladder. And when he knew all was set he puts the ladder agin the gable and climbs up with the corpse on his shoulder and he knew the gentleman was in the kitchen below waiting with a gun to level him, and he lets the corpse down the chimney. The minute it lit in the grate the gentleman let blarge with the gun and the shot knocked the corpse sideways.

'You killed him,' says the gentleman's wife; 'you'll be hung for murder. You better bury him at once.'

So she went on back to bed and the gentleman got a spade and threw the corpse on his shoulder and away out to bury him and left the door open, and in a while this gallows thief of a codger slips in and into the room and into the bed beside the gentleman's wife. And he rolled up the sheet in-inunder him and in a while says:

'I'm founded with the cold out burying that fella. Change places for a while.'

So when she changed over he rolled the other end of the sheet up, and then let on to go down for a drink or something and took the sheet with him and out and away.

The next thing in it he was to steal the horses out of the plough on this man ploughing, and the man would know he was coming and had a gun on the plough. So he goes and digs out this half-dozen or so young rabbits from this burrow and gets behind the ditch where the man was ploughing and lets the rabbits out into the field. When the man ploughing seen the rabbits he stopped the horses and lifts the gun and lets blarge, but the other rabbits were running here and there and over the ditches and he followed them. And the codger slips over the ditch and looses out the pair of horses and away with them.

That faired very well. The next thing laid out for him by the Old Thief was the hardest of all: he had to steal a sheep on the Old Thief himself.

'And I'll have it on a lead,' says he, 'and I'll be coming along such and such a road and watching out for you, and I'll have a gun and if I get me eyes on you I'll level you.'

What does the codger do? Slips into the town and whips a new pair of boots - that was no trouble to him at all - comes back, and at a bend in this part of the road he drops one of the boots, and round the bend he drops the comrade of it and gets behind the ditch and waits for the Old Thief coming with the sheep on a lead.

Along comes the Old Thief with the sheep and he meets in with the new boot lying on the road and of course picks it up.

'Damnbut,' says he, 'that's a powerful great boot if only I had the comrade of it; but sure what good is one boot.'

And he throws it down and goes on. Around the turn of the road he comes on the other boot and picks it up.

'Damnbut,' says he, 'this is the comrade of thon other boot: I'll go back for it.'

So he ties the sheep to a whin bush and goes back down the road around the turn and the codger hops out from aback of the ditch and takes the sheep. When the Old Thief come up and seen the sheep gone he was as mad as hell and says to himself:

'I'll buck him yet.'

And he goes back the way he come to get another sheep and let on it was the only one and he comes back like the fires of hell, and when he comes to this place where he'd lost the first sheep the codger was hiding in some whins and he started to 'meh-meh' like a sheep and says the Old Thief:

'Hell roast me skin but there's the other sheep where he has it tied.'

And he ties the second sheep to the whin bush along the road and away up the hillside and into the whins thinking to find the first one, and the codger hops out again and steals the second sheep.

And that was that. He could teach him no more. He was a better thief nor himself.

64. A Sort of a Clift*

Billy and Sammy went for a woman, and Sammy was a sort of a clift: it was Billy wanted the woman and Sammy was to do Blackfoot for him. And it appears Sammy had a wild appetite. So Billy says to him:

'Now don't disgrace me when you sit down to ate in this house: don't ate too much. As soon as I press your foot don't ate another bite, and even if they force you don't ate: say you've

* 'Clift' is a Tyrone term for a simpleton.

had enough. Let them see we know something and have some manners.'

The two went off anyway to this house where they were to get the woman and they were made welcome, and they were at the table eating. And what was knocking about the kitchen only this big greyhound dog and it got under the table and walked on Sammy's foot. So he wouldn't ate another bite though they forced him all roads up and across. But it was no use: he wouldn't lip a thing.

They were to be put up for the night, and when they went to bed there was light in Sammy's eyes with the hunger, wild with hunger. And Billy knew he would be. So says Billy:

'When all is quiet down below you can slip down. I seen the old woman of the house leave a bowl of sowans [a type of gruel made from the husks of oats] on the dresser, and take that take that and ate your fill.'

So Sammy slipped down; and whatever sort of a clift he was and he must have been a right clift, but in the dark he got the bowl of sowans and was coming back with it and missed the way, and where hell did he go but into the room where the old woman of the house and her man were sleeping, and Sammy tripped going up the bed and spilled the bowl of sowans between them. The woman wakened and lit a light and seen what was in the bed.

'Well, you dirty dog you,' says she to her husband, 'to go and do number one in the bed.'

And he turned round and blamed her and the row riz. By that time Sammy had slipped out and back up to Billy with the empty bowl.

So the woman got up and went down to the kitchen to clean herself and get something to clean up the bed, and Sammy was still wild with the hunger. So Billy says:

'There's a jug of milk on the dresser below. Slip down again and get it and that'll do you till morning.'

Down Sammy goes again, poking in the dark, and doesn't he ram his hand into the milk-jug and couldn't get it out. So he goes up to Billy and shows him what is wrong.

'Go down,' says Billy, 'and break it agin the porch of the door and you'll get your hand out.'

So Sammy goes down again, and the old woman was somewhere around the porch trying to clean herself, and Sammy breaks the jug agin her face. She roared meel-a-murder that it was thieves they had in the house, and riz the house, and hardly give the two boys time to put on them and yock up their horses and get away.

So the two boys started for home, and they come to a place where a man was sowing oats in a field. Billy says to Sammy:

'Go down and ask that man if he'd give us as much oats as would give a feed to the horses, and offer to pay for it. And say that you're the boy that hopes he'll have ten heads of corn next year where he had one the year.'

Down goes Sammy and asks for a feed for the horses.

'I'll give you a feed surely,' says the man.

'We'll pay for it.'

'I'll take no money off you,' says the man.

'That's more than good of you,' says Sammy. 'That you may have one head next year when you had ten the year.'

'Well, you damned clift you,' says the man, 'after me offering to give you a feed of oats free. Get to hell out of my field,' he says and lifts a graip and chases Sammy away to hell round the field.

So when Sammy came to Billy, Billy asked what happened.

'I said what you told me,' says Sammy. 'When he offered to give me the oats I said I hoped he'd have one head next year when he had ten this year.'

'Oh you clift you,' says Billy. 'But never mind.'

They went on and they met a funeral, a very sad funeral of a young girl that had died. And Sammy says: 'That you may have ten funerals next year where you had one the year.'

And that time they just got away with their lives.

'Why did you say a thing like that?' says Billy. 'Why didn't you say: "Lord have mercy on the corpse"?'

So the next thing they come to was a bridge and these men were hanging a dog.

'Lord have mercy on the corpse,' says Sammy.

The two men made for them and again they had to fly.

'My God,' says Billy, 'why did you say a thing like that? Why didn't you say: "Look at the two men hanging the bitch?" Remember that now.'

The next thing they see, or come to, was a church and there was a wedding at it; and whatever happened the bride was coming out hanging on to these two men: they were sort of holding her up in their arms.

Says Sammy: 'Oh, look at the two men hanging that bitch.'

That time they had to fly altogether. And that seems to be the end of the story ... Or all that was known of it round here in Glenhull. But it seems to me that whether it was or not Billy was as big a clift as Sammy. There was a pair of them in it!

65. They'll Force You To Take Soup

There was another man on the roads one time. Pat Loy they called him, and he come to this place and asked for shelter. He wasn't what you'd call by any means a bright man; but sure he had to live and get a bite to ate and a place to fire himself down at night like another.

Anyhow, when he knocked the door and told his errand, he was told he was welcome to stay, but if he wanted to get a bed he'd have to lie with a sick man. Pat said that would do him fine. Next they told him they hadn't a bite of supper except 'Blind Soup': that's soup made off vegetables and no meat in it. They asked him would he take some and he said he wouldn't bother, and they forced [entreated] him to take some and he said he didn't like soup.

So he got into bed and he shoved the sick man over to the wall and moved into his place and went as sound asleep as the bells. But what the hell, wasn't there a nurse of some kind attending the sick man during the night, some neighbour you understand, and it seems she had to give him some sort of injection: that's what they'd call it now, but that's not what it was then. Of course she knew nothing at all of Pat getting a night's shelter and I suppose anyway she was up out of her own bed and the sleep still in her eyes.

Anyway Pat was up at the screak of day and away like hell without waiting for anything to ate; and a bit further up the road he fell in with a man like himself who wanted to know where he would be safe to ask for a night's shelter.

And Pat says, telling him the house: 'You'll have to sleep with a sick man.'

'That's no odds,' says this fellow.

'But,' says Pat, 'they'll force you to take soup. And for God's sake take it,' he says; 'for if you don't this big strappin' girl will appear during the night from somewhere and will put a tin whistle up your backside and try to make you take it that way.'

66. The Tramp and the Foal

This was supposed to happen to a man the name of Quinn and I heard it told and it was no cod either; it happened.

He had a mare and foal and this morning a tramp come along and seen him with the mare and foal. He give the tramp something.

'I wish you luck of your foal,' says the tramp.

'Thank you,' says Quinn.

'But there'll be trouble over the same foal,' says the tramp.

'How could there by any trouble over that foal,' says Quinn, 'and him mine?'

'Well,' the tramp says, 'I'd put a mark on him. I'll do it if you like and you can see.'

Quinn sayed very good and the tramp says:

'Have you a silver thrupenny bit?'

Quinn looked his pockets and had nothing and he says:

'Hold on and I'll slip down to the house and get you one.'

He slipped down to the house and got a thrupenny bit and come back and give it to the tramp. The tramp then asked Quinn for the loan of his knife. He takes the knife and at the star on the foal's forehead he made a cut and just lifted the skin and slipped the thrupenny bit inside and pulled the skin over it again.

Quinn reared the foal and broke it in and had him carting one day in Dundalk: and be the holy fortune these two fellows come over and told him that he was carting with their horse. He denied it to be sure, but no good - they had him arrested and he wouldn't be bailed out, his word wouldn't be taken: they had day and date and description of the horse and said it was theirs.

The morning of the court come anyway, and it come back to him about the tramp. So he said in the court he had a private mark on his horse. The horse had to be got and he opened the mark at the star and took out the thrupenny bit. So he was let free then and the other two fellows were lifted and they put in time in jail for it.

67. The Man with the Bar of Gold

There was this man here in The Glens of Antrim one time and he got down in the world. He had a wife and family and a right farm of ground, but you know how it is - he lost heart. Things went from bad to worse, stock dying and what not, till he thought there was nothing for him and the wife and family but to turn the key in the door and take the high road for it.

This winter's night anyway with snow out him and his wife were sitting at what spark of fire they had when this rap come to the door: they always said he was a good-living man and that his misfortune wasn't all his own fault. He answered the door, and here was this old man looking a night's shelter and a bite to ate.

So he was made welcome as always, and whatever little they had they gave him a share of it. He was an old man and they said you wouldn't give tuppence for every stitch he had on him.

They sat cracking a while, and the old man seen there was something wrong and asked what was up. So they told him ... The world was agin them and they could do nothing about it.

'Maybe I could be of some help,' says the old man.

They give him no heed till here he takes out of the pocket of the old top-coat he had on him this bar of gold, pure gold. And he reaches it to the man in the house.

'Take that,' says he, 'and use what you want of it. But if I was you,' says he, 'I'd bury it now under the hearth-stone till you find you need it. And I'll be back in a year or so and whatever you have left of it, well and good.'

So they thanked him and buried it under the hearth-stone. Morning come and the old man got a share of what they had to ate and gathered himself for away, and the minute he was through the door there was neither hilt nor hair of him.

Well, the man in the house took heart, and with one thing and another plucked up courage and started again and got on the best at all. The world began to flow in on him. Until coming on this snowy winter's night some time after here this rap comes again to the door, and who is it but the old man. Well, he was made more than welcome and taken in and given the best in the house.

'I'm glad to see you thriving so well,' says he, and he asks him about the bar of gold.

And says the man of the house: 'Well, from the night me and you buried it there under the hearth-stone I've never laid eyes on it, and didn't need to.'

And neither he did: he only needed the bit of lift [encouragement] to put the heart back into him: there's no magic in the gold.

'Fair enough,' says the old man, and they dug it out again. 'I'll be on my way in the morning, for you never know what man like yourself might stand in need of it.'

68. The Castle on the Cuiltiagh Mountain

There was two brothers and they lived in Guberveeny [townland in Killinagh Parish, Co Cavan] and they were the name of McLoughlins; and one of them was a thatcher, and of course a thatcher that time was a very important man, because very few could thatch, and the other man was a great creel-maker.

They collected a few pound and they decided this time they'd go to races at Navan; they'd never seen races. So they struck off and headed out across the top of the Cuiltiagh Mountain. And when they went a certain distance out the mountain there came in a mist, and they decided it would be very dangerous to go any further.

'We might get lost in a bog-hole or a lake or something, and we'll just sit down and maybe it'll clear away.'

So eventually anyway they sat down, and away in the distance they saw this wee blue light.

'Well, I wonder now? It must be some man after sheep with a flash-lamp. Looking for sheep.'

So it lifted a wee bit and they got up and they started [to] tap the ground in case they'd get lost do you see ... Up on the top of the Cuiltiagh Mountain. So, as they went on it was getting brighter, this blue light, and brighter ... and brighter, and they kept moving on. And to their great surprise wasn't there a great big castle on top of the Cuiltiagh Mountain.

So, they thought this was a fret [fright: marvel], a wonderful thing to see on the top of the Cuiltiagh Mountain. So they said:

'We'll ring the bell.'

Everything was there in them days, there was a bell over your head. And this lovely lady appeared at the door.

'Oh, good morning. I suppose you two boys are getting lost in the mist.'

'Well, that's the truth, we were lost surely in the mist.'

'Oh, come in: yous look very cold ... You'll have a cup of tea.'

They were surprised. So they went in ... Aw, carpets and everything, a very beautiful place: it was no time till she had a lovely cup of tea made for these two boys; they were delighted with themselves.

Anyway, when they had their tea finished she came back in and she says:

'Tell me this, yous boys now: where did yous plan to go, or what have yous up here on this mountain?'

'Well, do you know to tell you the truth, Miss, we intended to go to the races in Navan: we never was at horse racing and we'd like to see horse racing.'

'Oh,' she says, 'you'll be there. You'll stop here the night, in this house, you'll be well looked after.'

That was another shock to them. So she come back; had a lovely bed for them and everything; and in the morning she had them up at six o'clock, and she had a lovely breakfast and everything that could be put on the table was on the table. So:

'Now,' she says, 'boys, are you short of cash?'

'Well, we have just a few pound.'

'Well,' she says, 'if you haven't a few pound I can give you some money. And,' she says, 'there's a grey mare in the stable and a saddle and a red horse in the stable; and you'll take them two ... You'll ride them two ... Could yous ride horses?'

'Oh,' he says, 'we could ride horses; we often rode horses. We were well used to horses, riding horses.'

'Well,' she says, 'you're good men. Well now,' she says, 'they'll be ready now, the horses in the stable, saddle and bridle and all, and when you're finished now, your meal, you can just take the horses out and get aboard the two horses and you won't be too long till you'll be in Navan.'

More excitement to the boys do you see. They just took the horses when they had their meal finished and:

'Now,' she says, 'I'll tell you one thing: As soon as you go to Navan put them into a stable, and don't be in any hurry down to the race-course. Is any of yous a good jockey?'

'Aw, that boy there could ride a horse.'

'Well, you'll ride that grey mare and enter her in the first race.'

Got going the two horses ... Ah, sure they went like swallows; they were landed in Navan ... Didn't take them an hour to land in Navan ... Hardly touched the ground at all: over hedges and ditches. Landed into Navan: far too early for the races to start. Put the horses into a stable and put a lock on the door. Took a walk through Navan and had a look round and here and there and every place; didn't find the time passing away till they seen men coming out with horses here and there. They decided it might be time now ... It was two o'clock the first race. So they decided:

'We'll dodge up now to see how the horses is getting on.'

So they went up anyway, took out this grey mare and let the red horse stay inside; took out the grey mare and walked on down to the race-course, paraded her round till the time came: your man aboard and on to the race-course. The tapes was lined along, and there was several men from all over, Meath and every place was there, with powerful great horses. Well, the tapes went up and he went out like a swallow, and he was looking back to see were they coming, do you see. Ah, sure she walked it. Got his stake money, whatever the stake money was [the amount of it]. He looked at it ... ten or fifteen pound that time, that's a long time ago.

Aw, the horse-dealers and all came and got round them.

'Will you sell the grey mare?'

'I wouldn't sell the grey mare, because I'll tell you: she was a wee pet foal that I got when I was a youngster and I reared her up and I wouldn't take no money for her, and I wouldn't sell her.'

Well, anything in the world, only to sell that grey mare to these great horsemen.

No: they said they wouldn't sell. Come down and put her into the stable with the red horse. Give it a grain of hay and said:

'We'll go back again now as soon as we get a bit of a meal.'

They had a bit of a meal anyway; and when they had their meal taken they went back up to the stable to have a look at the two horses. Put the key in the door and opened it: nothing there. Gone; the horses gone. They said:

'I suppose they've gone back again to the Cuiltiagh Mountain.'

And still the lock on the door. Well, they thought it strange.

'Well, we done very well now. We'll go over now to England where there's great racing: we'll go over now to see the Grand National.'

'Well ...'

So they landed in England anyway; they were knocking about and up and down and they didn't know much about any place to stop. So they tapped this door anyway; it was a chancy place for to stop. So this maid come to the door.

'Could you keep two men for the night?'

'Oh, certainly,' she says; 'come in,' she says.

They went in and they had a cup of tea. There was an old dame sitting over in the corner, very old dame. They finished their meal anyway.

'Now,' she says, 'boys, where did yous come from?'

'We came from Ireland.'

'And where are yous going to?'

'We're going to see the Grand National. They say it's a wonderful great race the Grand National.'

'Well, good men,' she says. 'I suppose when you come from Ireland you know how to play a game of cards?'

Aw, sure they were delighted to play a game of cards, you know, to pass the time. So she had a wee box in the corner like this do you see; she took out a pack of cards out of a big cupboard was in the corner and the game started. Ah, Jasus, they were winning hands down; they hadn't place to put the money into their pocket; they were cleaning her! Played away and played away and begod didn't the tide turn, do you see, and she started to win: she'd fire [fling] the money like this into the wee box, the basket like this do you see, and she cleaned all off them. And begod they thought: if we made one grab at that ould box and out the door: made a grab at the box and here two uniformed men appeared at the door.

'Take your time, boys. Leave that down again.'

And they fired them out on the street. Penniless, bar a few

bob.

'Ah, hard lines ... Hard lines. Well we haven't the price of our way back now. We'll have to strike for the road to see can we get any bit of work at all that we'd get money to bring us back home to Ireland.'

Well, they wandered about and wandered about, and the next morning they took out a road, away out of the city and they came to a cross roads.

'Now,' he says, 'I'll go this way and you can go that way. And,' he says, 'if we ... We'll meet here in about six months' time.'

Well, this man went to the right, he didn't go too far until he met a man in a horse and trap. See? Pulled up the horse and says:

'You wouldn't be looking for work?'

'Well,' he says, 'I'd take a job; I'd be delighted to have a job surely. I'll take a job surely.'

'Well, sit in with me. I'm going in to town for some groceries, to the village.'

Sat into the trap anyway, and they had a couple of drinks, not much, just a couple of bottles of stout, and made the bargain and all.

'If you stop with me for six months I'll give so much a week, and you'll be well looked after.'

He went off home with his man, and he had a wonderful great time; he was a terrible nice man; they got on shocking well. And he was living in a wee ould thatched house and he had a wonderful great farm of land. And away in the corner of this farm of land there was a lovely big two-storey slated house, a beautiful looking place. So this day he says to the farmer:

'Tell me this,' he says; 'there's a lovely house over there and I'm looking at it every day when I'm working. Who owns that house?'

'It's mine,' he says.

'And that's a fret,' he says; 'you're living in this old thatched house. Why don't you live in that?'

'I couldn't live in it.'

'Why?'

'It's haunted,' he says: 'there's a ghost in that house at night: it's a sight to the wide world.'

He says: 'Would you live in it?'

'I definitely will stop in it; why wouldn't I?'

'Right.'

Well, that night they sailed down at eleven o'clock.

'Now,' he says, 'anything you want I'll give it to you.'

'Well,' he says, 'I want a bottle of whiskey; I want a shot-gun. Give me two cartridges, and a bottle of Holy Water. And I'll stop in it. I'm no coward.'

He went down with the farmer at eleven o'clock; the farmer bid him good-bye. He was in bed; and about twelve o'clock the door bursted open. Two men come in carrying a coffin, do you see, and left it down on the floor. Took this old man out of the coffin and started to whale him and batter him, and the roars of him was a fret. He was looking out at them.

'Dammit,' he says, 'it's not fair,' he says.

And pulled on his trousers. He jumped out, and he made into the two boys that was battering the old man; a hardy boy he was. They fought him till two o'clock anyway, and at two o'clock they bundled him into the coffin and absconded out the door.

The farmer was down the next morning, thinking that he might be dead, you know.

'Aw,' he says, 'how did you get on last night?'

'Not too bad: it was a wee bit rough,' he says, 'but I came through it all right,' he says. 'Two men come in carrying a coffin and took an ould man out and started to whale him. And I went out too and wanted to do the best I could. I bested them. The old man wasn't bad either; he was good too.'

'Well, come on up to the house,' he says, 'for your breakfast.' He says: 'You won't have a hand's turn to do the day. Have a good rest. Will you stop the night in it?'

'Well, when I done so well last night I wouldn't mind stopping the night.'

Right. At the same time they went down as far as the house, and the farmer bid him good-bye; he closed out the door, the farmer went home; and at twelve o'clock it went in again, the door, and four men come in, carrying the coffin. Took the old man out of the coffin and started to batter him, whale him.

'God,' he says, 'it'll be tougher the night than it was last night.'

And he took a slug [gulped a drink] out of the whiskey to give him a wee bit of spirit. He pulled his trousers on and tied his galloses round him and in to it. Well, between the two of them ... the old man was good and he was good and they kept the boys at bay. At two o'clock bundled him into the coffin and absconded out the door.

The farmer was down the next morning.

'How did you get on last night?'

'A bit rougher than the night before. There was four of them,' he says, 'last night, battering him.'

'You got out?'

'Aw, I did, I did, I did.'

'Would you chance it the night?'

'Well, sure, when I done so well I'll chance it the night.'

'Good man. Come up for your breakfast.'

The same: hadn't a hand's turn to do.

The next night back down again. And at eleven o'clock:

'Good night now. Do the best you can.'

The same time at twelve o'clock the door was bursted open and six men come in, carrying the corpse, left it down and took the old man out and started to whale him.

'Begod,' he says, 'this is tougher than it was.'

And he took a slug out of the whiskey like this, and lifted the bottle of Holy Water and he just done this you see with the Holy Water [held it by the bottom and splashed the Holy Water out of the bottle round the house] on the coffin. The six men absconded out the door and left the old fellow there.

'Ah,' he says, 'you're a fine man. Now,' he says, 'that's the way I'm abusing for the last twenty years, what you seen. And,' he says, 'you have freed me. I swore agin those men wrongfully when I was on earth. And,' he says, 'you have freed me. You've done a great job for me. I won't be bothered any more: you have broke the spell. Good man,' he says. 'Now,' he says, 'for your goodness to me, in that corner of the room there's a crock of gold. And in this corner here there's a crock of gold, and that's my son you're working with, and I'm his father.'

That was all right. He absconded just like a flash out the door, coffin and all.

Next morning when the farmer come:

'Well, how did it go?'

'God,' he says, 'I have news for you.'

Told him the whole story, about who they were beating and everything, and he said:

'That son of mine can live in this house and there'll never be a word in this house ...'

That was all right: told the farmer the whole tale.

'Begod,' he says, 'you're a powerful great man.'

So they lifted a few boards in the corner and there the crock of gold was there. Lifted another couple here and the crock of gold was there.

The farmer says:

'I'll run up to the house now for two bags [sacks] : we'll carry it up to the house.'

So they carried the gold up to the house, the two crocks of gold. So, had his breakfast and a good sleep that day. The next morning the big farmer told him:

'You stop with me as long as you like.'

'I don't think I will,' he says. 'We got on terrible well together now, but at the same time the horrors of this,' he says, 'will be in me mind and I wouldn't be content.'

He says: 'I have only one daughter,' he says, 'and you can marry her, and I'll give her to you if you stop with me.'

'Now,' he says, 'I'm very thankful for the offer, but at the same time I'd be thinking of this me whole life and I'd never be content: I'd like to go back to Ireland where I came from.'

'Well,' he says, 'it's too bad. I'm terrible sorry for to part with you. But,' he says, 'I'll tell you: Now,' he says, 'I have a horse in the stable,' he says, 'and we'll put the crock of gold on him whenever you intend to go.'

'I'll definitely go,' he says, 'because I just couldn't stick it.'

So anyway, put the crock of gold in the bag and threw it across the horse's back, like that.

He says: 'When you go to the city,' he says, 'you can leave the horse,' he says; 'the horse'll come back to where it came from; he knows the way well, he was often in the city before, the same red horse.'

When he came to this crossroads he got off the horse and he was waiting to see any sign of the brother, where he was supposed to be in six months' time at this crossroads. No sign of him. He was a kind of tired and he tied the horse to an ould bush do you see; he lay up agin the bank like this to have a bit of rest and he fell asleep. Well, when he woke up, horse, gold, all was gone: some robbers or something come and they had everything. He was penniless again, after all his riches, just a few pound in his pocket and that was all.

Hard luck ... hard luck ... hard luck. Tough lines.

'Well,' he says, 'what can be done?'

So he wondered about the road to see would he see any sign of the brother. And there was a lovely orchard just with the apples, big red rosy apples hanging out nearly out across the wall. And he put up his hand - he was thirsty - and he started to ate an apple. And the next thing begod horns started to grow on him and got stuck in the trees and everything. There he was going about like this with his head down, with the horns, like what would be on a reindeer. So he looked up through the branches.

'Glory be to God,' he says, 'this is a fret.'

But anyway he was that thirsty he put up his hand and he pulled down another apple and he started to ate it, and bejasus the horns started to fall off him.

'I know now,' he says; 'there's a good tree and a bad tree. Throt and I'll put horns on the ould lassie that took me money off me if I can get a chance,' he says.

He put the good apple in this pocket and he put the bad apple in the other pocket. He headed on for the city where this old lady lived that took the money off him, do you see. He went down to a Jew shop and he bought a wee attaché case and he got a false moustache. The Jewman says:

'What do you want these for?'

'I'm acting in a play,' he says; 'I want to camouflage myself.'

And a wee bowler hat, and a moustache. The Jewman stuck it on him and all, and curled it like this do you see, and of course you wouldn't know him from Adam. Ah well, the next thing was he went up to the house, tapped the door anyway.

'Please could you give me a cup of tea, Miss, or a wee bit of a meal?'

'Oh,' she says, 'come on in. Why not?'

She didn't know that he ever was there before. And the old lady was sitting in an armchair and she was asleep. So when he had his meal took he just left the money down, the price of the meal, and he left the apple down; and she wakened up and he just absconded out the door. She wakened up and she lifted the apple ... Ah, the horns got stuck in the ceiling and here she was with her head down; the maid come and the maid nearly died when she saw the horns stuck in the ceiling.

'Aw, my God me poor mistress.'

The ringing was for doctors and specialists to try to get the horns off her: they came in with crosscuts, hatchets ... everything that ever they could think of to get the horns off her: well, they might as well be cutting that wall there with crosscuts and hatchets.

He kept moving about you see in the distance, and afeared. And there she was and there she was: couldn't make a bit hand at taking the horns off her. He kept moving about, up and down do you see. Eventually he went up to the door and he rung the bell.

'I believe,' he says, 'there's an old lady in here with horns on her.'

'There is ... Come in, come in if you can do anything for the creature, you creature.'

'Well,' he says, 'I'll do my best.'

'Oh, for goodness sake ...'

He had a wee attaché case and he walked into the room.

'Now,' he says, to the maid, 'you move and don't come back,' he says, 'till I call for you.'

Here she was with her head like this and the horns up in the ceiling.

'I want to speak to you for a minute.'

'Oh, why wouldn't you speak.'

'Did you do any harm to anybody in your lifetime that these horns was put on you?'

'Ah,' she says, 'I did; I did.'

'Well, you'll have to explain it to me before I take the horns off you.'

'There was two fellows from Ireland, and an-damnbut I took the money off them with witchery.'

'That's what has the horns on you. Now,' he says, 'madam,' he says, 'what would you give to have the horns taken off you?'

'Anything you ask. Anything you ask, I'll give it to you.'

'Well, five hundred,' he says, 'is my fee for taking horns off;

I took horns off old ladies before several times. Well, madam,' he says, 'I have to blindfold you. So, I want the money left down there first and foremost on the table ...'

In case she would use the old witchcraft again on him, do you see, when she got the horns off; he hadn't a second apple, to put them on again. Well, she put up her hand and she opened this, and she took out a big purse; counted out five hundred pound do you see, and he got a blindfold, a handkerchief and bandaged her eyes like this do you see.

'Now,' he says, 'eat of this fruit,' he says.

One horn fell off her.

'Eat another.'

Another horn fell.

'Eat another.'

Took another, another horn fell.

'Are you satisfied now?'

'Oh, yes, thanks be to God. It's great ... It's great relief.'

'Well, eat away at that apple. When you have it finished now,' he says, 'maybe there won't be a horn on you.'

So he rung ... and kept the door like that ... and lifted his money and absconded out the door and arrived back in Guberveeny where he came from.

69. Jack and His Talking Cat

There was this man one time, and he had two sons. An' here doesn't he die all of a sudden, an' what the hell does the eldest son do but turn out he's young brother on the high road, an' all the poor divil had, or was allowed to take with him was the cat. So the poor fella sets out without a bite in he's stomach, him an' the cat. So here anyhow, he comes to this place at nightfall, an' he sets about makin' a house out of sods for himself.

In them days, y'see, all the animals could talk. Well, the poor fella was next thing to starvin'; but an dammit, here every night wouldn't the cat take in a wild fowl. Aw, a very uncommon sort of wild fowl that the big men [gentlemen] of the country would give their eye for.

An' wasn't there this big gentleman's house near by, and here an' dambut, the cat tuck one of the fowl up to him an' left it for him.

'Now, that's very kind of you,' sez the gintleman. 'Where did you get these? I never seen the like afore though I heerd of thim?'

'Well,' sez the cat, 'me master caught that on he's estate an' sent me up with it, for he thought you'd like it.'

'That's more that daycint of him then,' sez the gintleman. 'I must go an' see him soon.'

So every evenin' the cat tuck a fowl up to the gintleman an' here this evenin', doesn't the big fella say that he must visit Jack ... that was the boy's name ... the nixt day. So the cat heeled it home to the sod house an' told the whole pant [incident] to Jack.

Jack was in a helluva state. 'Why damn yer sowl,' sez he to the cat, 'how am I to see him an' the state o' me? He'll have me life. Shur I haven't a stitch o' clothes on me at self.'

'Ah, don't let that worry you,' sez the cat. 'The morra evenin' when he's about comin', let you go down to the revver [river] an' take aff you an' go in an' bathe. An' let all your oul' duds go with the flood, an' just lave the rest to me.'

So good enough, Jack done as the cat bid him, an' here doesn't the cat eye the big gintleman comin' in he's coach an' four. An' away he goes like the wheels o' hell to meet him.

'If yeh plaze sir,' sez he, 'me master wint in to the revver to have a bathe, an' if the flood didn't wash all he's clothes away, an' he's in no state to meet you.'

'Dammit, that's too bad,' sez the gintleman. So he turns to a servant an' sez he: 'Away back you ahead of me an' bring the best rig-out [of clothes] you can get an' give them to the cat's master. I'll come another time then,' sez he to the cat. 'The morra for sure maybe.'

So good enough Jack got the clothes, an' sez he to the cat: 'I'm in a worse fix now nor ever. He surely have me life the morra when he finds me out, an' him after givin' me the suit of clothes.'

'Lave that to me,' sez the cat.

An' here an' dambut wasn't there an oul' *cailleach* [hag] of a witch livin' not far away, an' doesn't the cat go up to her castle. An' she made him welcome.

'I heerd about you,' sez the cat, 'an' I'm wonderin' if all I heerd is true.'

'What did you hear?' sez she.

'I heerd,' sez the cat, 'you could change yourself into any shape you liked.'

'So I can,' sez she, 'without bother.'

'Now could you take on the shape of a bull.'

An' while you'd wink yer eye, she was there as a bull.

'Damn good,' sez the cat. 'Now how about a calf?'

An' she did. An' so on, till he went down through all the animals, gettin' smaller every time, till he asked her to change into a mouse. An' the minit she did, the cat lit on her an' gobbled her up.

So home he goes to Jack. 'Now Jack,' sez he, 'there's a witches' castle close by, an' it's all yours to go an' live in if you wish.'

'Aye, but what about the witch?' sez Jack.

'Aw,' sez the cat, tapping he's belly with he's paw, 'she's safe an' sound kickin' in there.'

So Jack did as he was bid. An' the next day he met the gintleman an' showed him over the place, an' he swore he didn't think the like ever existed in Ireland. As far as I know, the gintleman had a daughter, an' he made a match with Jack an' her.

70. The Tramp and the Ghost

A tramp was promised 'a lump of money' if he would agree to stay in a haunted house. He agrees. He has been provided with a good fire, with food, drink and tobacco, and is left alone. He bars the door.

Around midnight he takes off one of his boots. He is taking off the other when he hears a sound behind him. He looks ... and sees a tall, dark man hovering above him.

'You're alone,' says the stranger.

'Yes,' says the tramp, 'and as soon as I get this boot back on you'll be alone too.'

71. The Widow's Three Sons

Well, the story I'm about to relate now is about a widow woman. Her husband died and left her with three sons. Well, Paddy and John were very smart people, but Mick wasn't very smart.

Paddy went away to make a living because they got very poor. He travelled on and on till he come to three crossroads, and he didn't know which road that he'd turn to that'd get him employment. So he says:

'I'll chance this one.'

And he went on and he travelled on and on and he come to a big house, and when he went into that house he asked for ... would he get employment. So the man says:

'I'll hire you,' he says, 'till the cuckoo sings. And if ever one of us gets vexed first,' he says, 'a bit shall be taken off your tongue.'

So, the boy agreed.

The next morning anyhow he was sent out with two horses and a plough, to plough in the fields. And there was a greyhound let out, in front of him, and he had to plough as much as the greyhound would travel, which was a very hard task. So the poor fellow he was sent out without eating his breakfast, he'd have his breakfast when he'd come in. So the greyhound travelled over hills and round, he never got a sight of the greyhound after he left a hundred yards.

So about three o'clock he come in - Aw, mad with the hunger, and the man says:

'Did you plough as much as the greyhound run?'

He says:

'I never seen the greyhound, but I'm ploughing all day and I'm hungry; I'm not able to walk.'

'And are you vexed?' he says. 'You know the bargain,' he says, 'whoever got vexed a bit would be taken ...'

'Why wouldn't I be vexed?' he says; 'I didn't get my breakfast.'

'Out with your tongue.'

The poor fellow had to put out his tongue and a bit was taken off it, and he was sent away back home.

So when he come back home he couldn't tell them anything. The mother says:

'Well, have you any money?'

And all he could say was:

'Ub-Dub-Dub ...'

He couldn't talk.

So, they were in as great a need as ever.

The second son went out and he was as unfortunate as the first. He went on and he travelled on along, and didn't he take the same road and come to the same house as his brother was [in] there before. The same bargain went on.

'Hire with me till the cuckoo would sing. And whoever gets vexed first a bit off the tongue.'

So the poor fellow went through the same thing. The greyhound was let out; he never seen the greyhound more, and he went back in - he was a high-tempered fellow - he tossed out table and everything to get his breakfast.

'Are you vexed?' he says.

'Why wouldn't I be vexed,' he says,'I got no breakfast.'

'Out with your tongue.'

So, this tongue, a bit was taken off it and he had to go 'way back home; and the other brother when he went in that the bit was taken off and he says:

'Ub-blub-blub ...'

And he says:

'Ub-blub-blub.'

But the young fellow anyway he knew well, that he says they were unfortunate, that they met with ... that the two of them be to meet with the one person anyway. So he says:

'I'll strike out.'

He was supposed to be ... Well, he hadn't as much sense or wit as the others; he was regarded as the fool of the family.

He went out anyway, landed at the house ... the same house ... took the same crossroads, he was unfortunate anyway. But the man hired him till the cuckoo would sing, and whoever got vexed first they had to ... a bit would be cut off their tongue.

The greyhound was let out in the morning, and he says:

'This is the house,' he says, 'that my two brothers got the bit off their tongue.'

So when the greyhound was let out he had a big quilt of a stick in his hand [a cudgel] and he hit the greyhound across the head and he killed him, and he ploughed across him. He came back into the house in a half-an-hour and the man says:

'Did you do the work,' he says, 'that I ordered you to do?'

'I did,' he says; 'we do a lot more in our country.'

And he went out and he got his prize greyhound dead and crossed over with the plough.

'Aw, God, you have me ... you have me prize greyhound,' he says, 'killed.'

'Well,' he says, 'are you vexed?'

'Aw, not a bit,' he says, 'I'm not vexed.'

If he said he was vexed the bargain was the bargain!

The next day he says:

'Well,' he says, 'I want you to bring cattle from that island to the mainland here,' he says, 'without wetting their hooves: I want you to bring them without wetting their hooves.'

'Very good,' he says.

So he thought of what he would do. He killed every one of them, on the island, and he carried them across in bags and he landed them and the blood flowed into the little river. And when the farmer landed across:

'Aw,' he says, 'you have me robbed. All me cattle killed.'

'Well you told me to take them over without wetting their hooves,' he says; 'that's what I would have to do, I have it done.'

'Aw, you have me robbed.'

'And are you vexed?'

'No ... No, I'm not vexed,' he says.

'Well, that's all right,' he says.

'Well now,' he says, 'there's a friend of mine coming to my house,' he says; 'he's a great friend of the king's,' he says, 'and he's coming to my house,' he says, 'and you must have great stepping-stones,' he says, 'and the greatest light,' he says, 'that ever was known in this vicinity. And you'll do that,' he says; 'if you don't we shall not be friends; anything can happen.'

Says the servant boy:

'I'll do my best. I've done very good,' he says, 'in the past and I'll try to be as good in the future.'

'Very good.'

He went and he killed all the sheep he had, and he put them down as stepping-stones, just about a few feet from other. He carted all the hay, and about the time that this king's friend was to come to visit he made a bone-fire of all the hay, and he landed, and it was wonderful.

'Well,' he says, 'you're a great boy,' he says, 'the light was wonderful; and the stepping-stones,' he says, 'that he walked on there could be nothing better. Where did you get them?'

'Well,' he says, 'I killed all your sheep,' he says, 'and I

burned all your hay.'

'Aw my God,' he says, 'you have me robbed. What am I going to do?' he says. 'You have me robbed.'

'And are you vexed?'

'No,' he says, 'I'm not vexed. 'It's all right.'

They come to the conclusion to get redd of him, the young fellow was robbing them all days of the year from [since] he come there.

The old mother was alive, and the son says:

'You get up in that bush and sing "cuckoo".'

Because the bargain was he hired with him till the cuckoo would sing, and when the cuckoo would sing that he was to get his money.

So anyway the old woman, his mother, went up in the bush to sing 'cuckoo' and he was sent out to put slates on the roof of the house, the young fellow. So anyway she got up in the tree and ... Ah now she couldn't imitate the cuckoo very good, she was a wee bit hoarse.

So he looked over and he could see her old grey head between the branches; and he looked over and he says:

'Arra, go to hell,' he says, 'you're not the cuckoo, and it's not time for the cuckoo to sing.'

And he took a slate and he fired it and didn't he hit her in the head and she fell to the ground. The son came out - she was on the ground roaring and crying.

'You have me mother killed. God bless us,' he says, 'me mother is killed.'

'Aw well,' he says. 'And are you vexed?'

He thought for a while.

'No,' he says ... 'Aye, why wouldn't I be vexed,' he says, 'when you killed my mother.'

'Out with your tongue,' he says, 'till I get a bit off it.'

So the boy was trying to keep him to his bargain, because he knew what happened to his own two brothers, and the farmer, the man that employed him says:

'If you let me not have the bit off my tongue I'll give you two bags of gold and,' he says, 'you can go home.'

So the young fellow got his two bags of gold; went home to his mother and two brothers; and they all lived happy.

And indeed I was talking to them it's not three months ago, and they all lived happy!

8 TALES OF ENCHANTMENT AND WONDER

The storytellers: Mickey Joe Anderson

72. The Enchanted Island

I won't tell a lie: I heard of The Enchanted Island in Glenshesk in Ireland above Ballycastle before I came here to Rathlin Island. And I heard it told here on Raackery [Rathlin] too. What I'm telling now I heard here in Raackery from a Raackery man; all his peope were from Raackery. He was a man called Donald Ruagh from the Upper End of this island.

The second Tuesday in May and the second in November were Hiring Days in Ballycastle beyont in Ireland, and the farmers would go through the Fair and hire girls and boys to work for them. November was called 'The Winter Fair'.

Well, this girl was in the Fair and the man come hiring her: whether she was a Raackery girl I won't say for fear I tell a lie. Boys for Raackery would be hired for ten shillings the full term and a plaid, and the plaid was only a bag [sack] to keep the rain and weather off them when they'd be herding sheep and cattle from the brae heads.

But to go on with the story. This girl hired with this man and she left with him to go to his home and he took her in a conveyance he had. When he was well outside the town of Ballycastle he took a hood and put it over her head and told her not to be 'feert [afraid], and he kept the hood over her head till she reached the farmer's house: she never told afterwards where she was; I suppose she didn't know.

She reached the farmer's house and liked it; the farmer in the days and weeks after was more than good to her. Anyway when her six months (term) was up she was paid her wages and she said she was for going home. The farmer said he was for going with her, and did go, and he put the hood over her head again the same as when she came. He told her when she was leaving she was never to try to tell where she'd been and he warned her never to speak to him if she'd happen to run across him any place.

Well, that was all right. She got there and he took the hood off and she went home for a while. But she was in Ballycastle one day after and here she sees the same man that she was hired with. He was that good to her that she couldn't help running across to speak to him: she thought it would be a wild poor thing not to speak to such a man that had been so good to her.

And what did he do ...? He had a top-coat over his shoulder, and she spoke till him, and he looked wild angry and wanted to know what she wanted.

'Don't you mind I was hired with you and you were more than good to me?' she says.

And he lifted the coat off his shoulder and hit her a switch of it across the face and blinded her for life; they said she never saw a stime after.

Donald Ruagh told me, and others forby, about The Enchanted Island rising every seven years. And he said that if you could pick soil then when you saw it from under your left foot, sand or a pebble or anything, off the hard land, and be fit to throw it on The Enchanted Island, if you got time before it disappeared again it was to stay for ever above sea level. The Green Island was another name he had for it too.

I heard of a family up in Glenshesk was supposed to be ones of The Enchanted Island.

73. Lig Na Bayste

That means 'The Hollow of the Beast' and it's at the Lower End of the Island, and the people used to be 'feert to go through there one time. There was supposed to be an enchanted beast there; that's what the ould ones called it.

And they told of this man that went to face it. At the time the people done a lot of slaughtering of their own cattle on Raackery. This man got a bullock's skin and he went to the blacksmith and got him to make a lot of flat-headed nails. He drove these through the skin with the points sticking out. He got another skin and put it inside and got in himself and went to fight the beast at Lig-na-bayste. The Enchanted Beast met him and opened its mouth and took him into its jaws and went to close its mouth on him, but the nails stuck in it and he managed then to kill it. Neal used to tell that.

There was supposed to be another Enchanted Beast used come ashore out of the sea on to the Island, and they said that a McCurdy man married to a McCurdy woman could take any stick and kill it or release the person who had been turned into the beast.

74. The Woman from the Sea

There's a day they say when no one should go near the shore, let along put out in a boat to fish: that's when there was fishing along the shore here around Layde, in Red Bay and Cushendall.

And maybe that's how this fellow from here fell in with the mermaid. They say if you once heard her sing you'd never do a day's good after, thinking long on it. Anyway this fellow - I believe it was Conn they called him, a man living his lone at the time - he was up this Easter Sunday morning and was down at the brae-heads seeing to the sheep. There was one or two down at the shore, so he slipped down to turn them away from the tide with the lambs with them. And then he heard this woman singing, and then he seen the mermaid herself sitting on this rock a bit back from the water, and lying beside her was this *sloak*: a *sloak* they always called it; like a fish-tail that the mermaid pulls on when she goes into the water: all in dazzling colours of the rainbow and scales too: a lovely thing they said.

Well, before the mermaid seen him or heard him he was behind her and grabbed at the *sloak* and she grabbed and screamed, but it was no good. Conn had it and turned for home and she be to follow him.

They got married anyhow, and she wanted him to destroy the *sloak*: he wouldn't hear tell of it and said he would hide it. For she said that if ever she got her hands on it she would have to back to the sea. He hid it well in the thatch anyhow.

Well, time went on and there was two children, two cubs [boys] born to them. This Lammas time he was at the Fair in Ballycastle with cattle or sheep, and you know the Lammas Storm and floods we get. A wild storm riz when he was away and was lifting the roof off the house. So the woman got a rope and done her best to get it across the roof to hold it down and then the wind riz this lump of thatch and she seen the *sloak* and that was that.

When Conn got home the roof was near all off the house and the two cubs were roaring their heads off with fear and said their mother left them. And when Conn found the *sloak* gone he knew what had happened. Well, they say he went to the shore and called and called to her but he might as well have stayed at home. She never showed up and never returned.

But they used to say that many's the morning Conn would

find a rush basket of fish at the door, and many's the time when he was too tired to wash the two boys at night he'd find them tidy and clean the next morning, as clean as a sea-shell, only there'd be bits of scales of the *sloak* on them.

75. Visions of a Murder

There was a man one time here on the Island, John Craig, and he was a remarkable man. One time he was going down to fish at a place called Benmore here, and there's a wee hollow as you go down. It was just about that time of the evening when the sun would be setting: and in this hollow he saw an uncle of mine they called Angus McCuaig fighting.

There was a darkie fighting him, two men on my uncle, and one of them had a knife. John told it all and could have described each of them, and the sort of country it was, the hedges round it, and the kind of fruit on the trees. And he saw the darkie rise the knife and stab my uncle Angus in the breast.

Well, my father was alive at the time but he didn't say anything about it to him. He went to a grand-uncle of mine and told him, and says he:

'Did you not tell John about this?'- That would be my father.

He said he didn't. Angus McCuaig you'll understand was somewhere in America at the time.

'Well,' says my grand-uncle, 'you'll come down now and tell him.'

So he went down and told him all he had told my grand-uncle. My father then started to get in touch with Consuls and one thing and another but there was never any more trace of Angus; never was heard tell of.

Well, that very same night when my father went to bed he woke up and found Angus standing over him and him covered in blood, the way John Craig had described him. And my father leapt out of bed and ran up to my grandfather. He could have told him that Angus was seen running to the house as if there was someone after him. But no word was ever got of Angus.

The priest got to hear of it: John Craig himself told the priest about it; and the priest told him that if he hada went up when he saw them fighting in the hollow and spoke to them in the Name of God he could have saved Angus' life.

That's all true, believe it or not.

76. The Water Horse of Burren

There were very few horses at all in Burren [Co Down] at one time, and there was no stallions for miles and miles around. But this man anyway ... I think he was McDonnell ... he had a mare and he lived near the lake.

He was joined with another man, a horse a piece, and they were ploughing this day and the other man says to McDonnell:

'Begod your mare's in foal.'

'Not at all, man,' says he, 'how could she be in foal, I never had her served. And how could I have her served and not a stallion horse in the country?'

But the mare was in foal and she foaled, and the foal they said was the loveliest thing ever you seen. It would run like mad around the fields and crowds would gather from all over County Down to watch it. It was a great foal they allowed.

Anyhow, it come the time to sell and McDonnell was for selling the foal. And they said that this stallion put its head up out of the water in the lake in the bog and nickers ... neighs ... and the foal run and jumps into the lake and was never seen from that day to this.

I knew people who would swear all that happened and was as true as the sun shines.

9 WARRIORS AND GIANTS

The storytellers: Frank Craig, right, with his nephew

77. Oisin and St Patrick

Oisin's supposed to be buried there in Carnagore [South Armagh] where he come back to when he left Tir na n-Og: he was in fairyland and wasn't supposed to put his foot to the soil off the steed he was riding, but there was a woman there at Carnagore trying to lift a bag of turf-sods on her back and he just put his foot to the bag to help and touched soil and down he come, a done old man: he was years on top of years in Tir na n-Og and thought he'd only been a few weeks away.

Anyway, all the Fianna were dead and gone and that's where Oisin met St Patrick and St Patrick converted him. Sure didn't Patrick happen to let the sharp butt of his staff lie on Oisin's bare foot, and he didn't know it till he seen the blood and St Patrick's asked him why did he not complain: Oisin said he thought it was all part of the conversion.

78. Oisin and The Magic Bull

The time St Patrick met Oisin and converted him Oisin had turned into a very old man; and St Patrick was building his church at Armagh at the time.

But he was getting no further with the work; every blessed night this bull would come out of the woods and cowp [overturn] and scatter all they had built during the day.

Patrick was beat. And in the latter end he said his only remedy was to ask Oisin if he could do anything about this wild bull: Oisin was a giant of a man you understand, a powerful man altogether in his days with Finn and The Fianna before he went to Tir na n-Og [The Land of Youth].

Well, Oisin good enough heard the story, and he allowed he thought he'd be fit for the bull if only St Patrick would pray for him to have the strength of twenty men of that day.

St Patrick said he would, and away he goes to pray for Oisin to get the strength of twenty men, and the Lord heard his prayer and Oisin got the strength of the twenty men.

But it was no good: the bull came that night after Oisin bet it away and knocked and scattered what they'd built that day the same as usual.

So Oisin asked St Patrick to pray that he might have his old strength back again. And St Patrick went away and he prayed hard, and Oisin's former strength was given back to him, restored, the same as it was before he went to Tir na n-Og.

And that night he faced the bull again; and it was a long hard fight and in the end an - dammit he mastered the bull and the Divil's own fight he had to kill it.

But before Oisin killed the bull it seen it was at last meeting its match and when it could do no more it give a lep, a wild lep at Armaghbreague, and the track of its hooves is to be seen in the rock of the mountain there to this day.

Oisin killed the bull, but he was done out. So he skinned the bull and put the hide about him like a cloak and made his way back to where St Patrick had the masons building his church. He was that far through he could go no further, so he lay down with the hide of the bull about him, and in no time he was sound asleep.

The following morning early St Patrick's men come again to start at the building of the church: and there was Oisin, as sound as the bells, asleep and snoring.

Then St Patrick come up and he seen what had happened and Oisin asleep. He told the men for to creep up and by all and any means take the cloak off Oisin: he was afeared what might happen if Oisin awoke and the power still on him.

So they crept up. Oisin was still snoring; and he sucked the men up to him, and when he snored out with every breath he pushed them back again; in and out. And St Patrick seen it and the men, Oisin's snores sucking them in, his breath blowing them out: in and out, in and out.

There was only one thing he could do. He went away to pray; and if he prayed hard the first time for Oisin to get back his strength to beat the bull he prayed twice and three times as hard for the Lord to take the strength away from Oisin while he slept, for God only knows what notion Oisin might take into his head when he'd waken.

And St Patrick's prayer was heard.

79. Finn McCool and The Scotch Giant

Finn McCool was the tightest man in Ireland in his day, but he was heart afeared of this Scotch giant. And this day at Slie' Gullion he seen the Scotch giant crossing over The Mourne Mountains and out be Omeath coming to meet him. He was in a helluva way. Finn's wife was there, and Finn was for clearing off be Mullacrew or Tara but she seen he wouldn't have time and she told him to hop into the cradle in the kitchen and to hap himself well up: there was cradles in me own day and I seen butts of men sleeping in them, but they were half drunk.

Finn got into the cradle. His wife was making a bonnick of bread at the time, and she lifted the griddle off the fire and put it in the middle of the bonnick and threw the cake of bread in a scouder across the tongs on the fire when the Scotch giant walks in.

Where was Finn?

'Aw,' says she, 'he left a while ago to go hunting up be Mullacrew or Tara.'

Would he be long? That'd be hard to tell.

'I come to fight him,' says he.

'You could get more than your fill,' says she.

She asked him then was he hungry after his journey and he said he was and she threw him the bonnick with the iron griddle in the middle. He give a bite at it and sunk his teeth in it and the griddle didn't leave a sound tooth in his head.

'Is that what Finn ates?' says he.

'He wouldn't thank you for half-a-dozen of them,' says she.

So the Scotch giant began to think it was time he was making himself scarce. He sees the playboy in the cradle.

'Who's this?' says he.

'The youngest,' says she.

'Has he teeth yet?' asks the Scotch giant.

'Why don't you run your finger into his mouth and see?' says she.

He done that, and Finn took finger and all off him.

So begod he says to himself when Finn ates bonnicks like that and his youngest child can bite off a finger it was time to be making tracks, and he cleared away hell home to Scotland.

80. Finn McCool and the Cailleach Bhiorra

The Cailleach Bhiorra lived above on the top of Slie' Gullion and she was a witch, and she could turn herself into anything when she wanted to go through the country. She used to turn herself into a deer or a stag and Finn would be out hunting and would chase the stag and was never fit to catch it. And he had a great pack of dogs and the best of them was one they called Bran.

He used to rise this deer above near Mullacrew and it would run like the wind down through The Gap of the North here and into the bushes - this country in South Armagh was all bushes then - and that'd be the last Finn would see of it.

So he laid some sort of a trap this day. And when they riz the stag he managed to turn it, and as far as it was told the stag had to run up through Ravensdale and Annaverna and up the mountain and Finn's dog Bran on its heels. Finn followed it as hard as he could, and here he comes on Bran - stone dead: maybe that's where they buried him, at Carnamadda on Ravensdale mountain.

But Finn tracked the deer some way or other and away up Slie' Gullion and he lost the track up there. He come as far as the lake on Slie' Gullion, and here was this hellishin fine looking young woman sitting on one of thon mill-stones that's above at the lake, and her crying like the rain. Finn didn't know her from Adam.

He asked her what she was crying for, and she said she'd lost this ring; whether she said she was married or single I don't mind, but this was an awful valuable ring and she'd be foothering with it and it dropped into the lake.

So he asked her where and she told him, and without another word in goes Finn into the lake and dives down, but damned the sight of ring or thing could he see, and he was more than lucky to be able to swim up and out: and when he come out he was a done old man and his hair was as white as snow. There was no sign of the fine young woman, but only this old cailleach of a one and her laughing her length at him: it was The Cailleach Bhiorra all the time. - She'd changed herself into a young woman. She was fed up with Finn chasing her and now he was hardly fit to stand. So she seen Finn's men coming and she dives into the lake herself and that was that.

Finn's men come up and didn't know a bit of him, only one of Finn's dogs run and leapt and smelled around him and when Finn told his story they knew he was telling the truth.

The job then was what were they to do? But some one of them advised them what to do: to dig down alongside the lake and hoke the Cailleach out. But when they started to dig it was all solid rock. So they had to go back apiece, and back apiece, and had to keep going back till they come to where The Cailleach Bhiorra's House [a chambered cairn on the summit of Slieve Gullion] is the day, and they were fit to dig down there. And they sort of made a tunnel with big flags as they went until they were right up agin the lough and ready to drive a bar through.

And then the Cailleach herself come up and shouted at them to stop, or the lake would flood through the hole and drown Ireland. So they made her give back Finn his youth again and she did, but she wasn't fit to change the colour of his hair.

And from that day till the day he died Finn McCool had white hair.

81. A Meeting of Two Giants

A giant in Munster heard of a giant in Ulster and set out to meet and kill the Ulster giant.

When they met the Ulster giant says: 'Yesterday I killed seven with one blow.'

The Munster giant decided he had heard enough and at once set back for Munster.

The Ulster giant didn't tell him that it was seven flies he had killed!

82. He Made the Giants Fight

This young fellow was going along the road to seek his fortune, and this was the time of the giants. Travelling along this road he seen three giants building a bridge. He filled his pockets full of wee stones ... they didn't see him ... and he climbed up in a big tree. The three giants was working at the bridge and he joined [began] to throw a stone at them. And he hit one of the giants with a stone. The giant looked round and he seen nobody. He says:

'It was you hit me,' he says to the other fellow. 'Now don't do it again.'

Well, the young fellow fired another stone and he hit the giant. And the giant turned and says:

'I told you not to do it again.'

And he hit the brother and begod he killed him, he killed

the brother.

'It was you was throwing the stones; it was you was the cause of it and I'll kill you.'

And he killed the other fellow. Begod he killed the two brothers.

And the lad jumped down out of the tree; he had an ash-plant with him. And the giant says:

'It was you done it all. I'll kill you.'

'No,' says the lad, 'you will not. I tossed [knocked] a chapel the day and I killed the priest and thirty of a congregation, and I'll kill you,' he says to the giant.

The giant got afraid of him.

'Aw no,' he says, 'you'll not. Come up to the house,' he says. 'Come on.'

Brought him up to the house, up to the giant's house; and there was a big feast got ready for him. The giant wanted to test this fellow to see what he was. He says:

'We have to go to the wood for a tree,' he says.

'All right,' says the lad.

Went to the wood, and the big tree was cut, branches and all. The young fellow says:

'You get in to that end of it,' he says; 'I'll take the big end' ... that was the top and the branches and all.

The two got in under the tree, and of course the giant carried the whole tree: the lad was only on top of the branches. Landed above at the house.

A big feast got and of course the giant ate about half a bullock or something.

The giant says to him then:

'We have to go to the river to bring water out of the river.'

Ah, he had two big barrels and they were an awful size, carrying them.

'Ah,' says the young fellow, 'I'd bring that water to the house with me without carrying it at all. Yous are horrid fools,' he says, 'to be carrying water out of the river. I'll bring it to your house and you won't have to carry it at all.'

'Will you do that?' says the giant.

'Get me a spade,' he says.

So the giant thought he might bring up the whole river and drown him.

'Aw,' he says, 'we'll leave it there. We'll bring no water at all.'

Well, the giant and his mother were living there in the house and the giant and his mother planned they'd kill the fellow that night. Brought in a big flail ... Aw, a powerful big flail, an iron flail. The lad wasn't sleeping at all. And there was a calf in the room, and they had a mind to kill the fellow after he was in bed awhile - he wasn't sleeping - and he got out of the bed and he got the calf and he put the calf into the bed, and he got outside inunder the bed.

And the giant and the mother come up to the room to kill him with this big flail, and she had a light lit.

'Hit him,' she says.

And of course the calf let a roar.

'Hit him again.'

And the lad under the bed let a moan.

'Hit him again,' she says, 'for to make sure.'

He let another big moan.

'Now he's dead,' she says to the giant.

They went down to the kitchen and they were talking. The lad come down out of the room.

'Aw,' he says, 'I was dreaming,' he says. 'I was dreaming an awful dream,' he says. 'I thought three hailstones fell on me breast,' he says. 'It was yous,' he says, 'and yous were going to kill me, and I'll kill yous now.'

'Aw,' the giant says, 'no; we'll give you as much money as you're able to carry away.'

'Aw,' the lad says, 'I'll never ask that much. I'll only ask what you'd be able to carry,' he says to the giant.

So the giant ... there was a big bag of gold filled for him, and he carried it across the river.

'There now,' says the lad; 'I'll bring it the rest of the way myself.'

So he lived happy all his life after.

83. A Terrible Strong Man

The Feeack was a giant: a terrible strong man. He was in the fight at the Battle below Crocka-screedin: that's the Hill of the Screaming where the women of Raackery one time watched their men being slaughtered in battle.

This time there was three men there fighting agin an army: so the old ones would say here. The Feeack was badly wounded and he made his way up the South Side and with the wound he got his guts were coming out and he was stopping and pushing them in again; another few yards and his guts were down at his feet again; and the Raven was after him all the time and was for pulling the guts from him and he'd have to gather them and put them in again and hold them with his hand.

He got away anyhow, a desperate strong man and he was at Crockcoolin: that's the stone they say was flung from Knocklayde. The soldiers tracked him to there with the blood, and he got his back to the rock and they were 'feert to face him. It's as high as a man's head. And whatever way they managed it they got at him from behind: one soldier got up on Clockcoolin and threw a stone down on Feeack's head and killed him.

10 THE BLACK ART

The storytellers: Neil Craig

84. Harry Stotle's Black Book

That Black Art's worked by the power of the Divil and there's not a word of lie in it; it could be done - and can still be done: I read in a paper the other day a priest in Dundalk preaching that it could be done.

There was several ways of doing it - a man would sell himself to the divil and be free for seven years and then the divil would come to claim him, but he could make the divil sweep the bottom of the seven seas for him before he'd go, till the money would be pouring out of the tops of his boots.

There was someway of swearing on an anvil in a blacksmith's forge; sure Willy the Wisp in the first place was a blacksmith that sold himself to the Divil and beat him in the end. And they could hold up the Ace of Hearts at the Consecration of the Mass and they'd have The Black Art. And they could gather the seeds of the bracken on black plates at twelve o'clock on Hallow Eve Night. And you could read some book that come from foreign parts: it was a book with black pages and white writing and you read it from back to front and from right to left. And it warned you:

'Read me through
Peruse me not
Or Hell's fire
Will be your lot.'

That was the book they said of Harry Stotle [Aristotle]. I heard of men that sold themselves to the divil. There was two of them in this parish of Dromintee. One of them had only to think of a thing and it happened. One time they said he was watching Stephen McDonald's ones putting pork in the cart one Thursday morning for Newry market. Says he to the mother standing by:

'Wouldn't it be quare fun if they weren't fit to get the pigs into the cart?'

And damn-me if they could: nor half the country could lift the pigs into the cart.

Another time coming out of Newry he went into the last pub for a drink and there was a barmaid in it. Whether she said he had enough as it was or whether he passed some remarks out of place, she said he'd get no drink. The bar was full. Says he to her:

'For two pins I'd leave you standing on your head on that counter.'

No sooner said nor done. Before the whole bar she was up on her head and who the hell was fit to get her down ...?

Sure when he'd be out rambling at night and neighbours would be in cracking with the mother, she'd know when he was coming home, and where he was at. The plates would start to rattle first.

'He's turning at the cross now,' she'd say.

Then the plates would start to hop and dance and hell knows what else.

'He's at Jemmy's now,' she'd say.

Half the kitchen would be hopping by the time he walked in the door.

Well, he'd read some book and a helluva job he had to get shut of it. Some priest ... I think it was a silenced priest: they have more power than ever before ... I think a Father Duggan relieved him. He was to go and take the book and bury it at a point where three counties met and no matter what happened when he was burying it he wasn't to look behind him. The first time he tried to bury it a big black dog appeared out of nowhere with fire in his eyes and him spittin' sparks and made a lep for the ball of his leg. He had the last spadeful to throw in the hole where he'd buried the book when the dog made the charge and he looked round; and there was the book back in his pocket. The priest read and sent him a second time another night and when he was about to throw in the last spadeful he thought Slieve Gullion fell behind him and looked round and the book was back out of the hole in his pocket.

I forget now what happened the third time. But he got shut of it and cleared body and bones out of this country altogether.

85. The Horn Was Off the Cow

There was this widow woman here in the County Antrim and she had one brave good farm of land and wanted another for she had a houseful of daughters. The daughters were no way good-looking and she wanted to get them off her hands: so she knew she be to give them a farm apiece or a divide of her own. And there was this old man lived beside her and she wanted to get her hands on his farm of land.

He was the sort of man that was fold of playing cards and taking a drop of drink: he had no woman of his own understand, never married at all. But he was fair getting through his money, and with the drinking and the late nights card-playing and not looking after himself he was bad with pains.

So this day he says to her.

For why should he work and be killing himself if she would take the farm and give him his meat and a trifle of money when he wanted it and she could have the farm.

If he got real bad he'd have one of the widow woman's girls to look after him: that was the idea: a canny old boy that lived somewhere above Glenshesk or Loughguile or that way.

And says the widow woman to him:

'For why would you work,' she says, 'and you bad with pains? Give me the farm and I'll feed and bed you and give you all the oaten-bread and milk you want.'

So she got the farm off him and fed him for a couple of years, and he had a healthy appetite and no worry now, and he was away playing at the cards till all hours with the boys. But he run into a spell of bad luck, so then he joined [began] to look for a trifle of money off the widow woman.

'Give me twenty pounds,' says he.

'Aw,' says she, 'sure I fed you for nothing for long past. You've over-ate the price of your piece of ground.'

It went to law, and she bate him at the law and he was worse off than ever. And says he to himself: 'I must make a plan.'

And he made a plan with the young fellows he was playing cards with; and the plan was to say that he had the 'blink': could blink [overlook] a cow or a horse-beast or anything: they put it out he had The Black Art all the time. They told the widow woman he had The Black Art but she said she didn't give a damn for the blinking, she wasn't afeert of him or it.

So they made this plan. The plan was for the young fellows to steal one of her cows and take the cow and hide her away in a glen and tether her there. They done that; but they knocked a horn off the cow taking her to this glen in the dark.

Well, the widow woman missed the cow and she had the

daughters looking for the cow but they couldn't find her. So she went to the old man and rapped him up out of bed.

'You stole my cow,' she says.

'I stole none of your cow,' says he; 'I didn't know she was stole.'

'Well,' says she, 'I heard you have The Black Art; I heard what you can do. I want her back,' she says.

'Well,' says he back till her, 'if I take her back would you find it hard to give me oaten bread again and a drop of milk and a trifle of money?'

Well, she didn't know; she'd see. But could he tell her first where the cow was. Says he:

'It'll be a very hard job to find her.'

'All right,' she says, 'I'll give you oaten bread and milk. Come up to the house.'

'It'll be a very hard job,' he says; 'I'd need a taste of whiskey as well.'

Up the widow woman went and sent a daughter for a bottle of whiskey and come back with it and up to the old man and he drunk a good taste of it.

'Take more if it'll help,' she says; 'if it'll hurry the cow back, take another taste.'

He took a good slug. He was taking another when she stopped him.

'That'll do till you find me cow.'

'Oh, a very hard job,' he says.

Well, he got an old book and let on to be reading some gibberish out of it and made a sign or two, and he started to sweat ... the whiskey was working.

'I told you it would be a hard job,' he says, and he joined to wipe more sweat off himself ... the whiskey understand.

'I see your cow,' he says.

'Where?' says the widow woman.

'Your cow,' says he, 'is in a glen just bordering on Clough-mills.'

'As far away as that?' says she.

'I'm bringing her back,' says he.

He let on to make more signs and sayed some gibberish.

'Clough-mills,' says she.

'No,' he cuts in, 'she's at Antrim town now ...'

'Do you want to bust the cow?' she shouts. 'Drive her azy or you'll kill her.'

And says he: 'She's lost a horn as well as being tethered in thon glen ...'

And he told her where she'd find her cow, and so the widow woman and a few of the daughters went out and got the cow tethered in the glen not far away and took her home and tied her in the byre. Next morning she come and rapped the old man up again. And says she:

'You were fit to find the cow. So you can put on a horn then?'

'A very hard job,' says he.

'I'll give you milk and oaten-bread while you live,' says the widow woman, coaxing him: the loss of the horn would spoil the look and sale of the cow: she couldn't fortune her off either with one of the daughters. 'I'll give you oaten-bread and milk while you live,' says the widow woman.

'I'd want more,' says he; 'a very hard job to put a horn on a cow.'

So she said she'd send for more whiskey.

'I'd need that and more,' says he.

'You have The Black Art,' says the widow woman; 'you can do it if you want.'

He said this was the hardest job in the world. In the end she made a bargain to give him more money, so much a week and his keep. So she got him another taste of whiskey and told him to get on with the job: she wanted to see that horn back on the cow.

'While I'm on the job,' says the old man, 'you're not to speak or all my hard work will be lost.'

'I'll not speak a word then,' she says.

'Very good,' says he. 'Bring up the cow.'

One of the daughters brought up the cow and he joined to sweat ... the whiskey working again and she said indeed it was a very hard job, and he joined to put more gibberish out of him.

'You won't speak now?' says he and the sweat blinding him.

'I won't,' says the widow woman; 'get on with your work.'

He put more gibberish out of him. And says he:

'One horn ...'

The widow woman didn't speak a word. He waited a while; and he had a stick, a rowan tree, a Gentle Bush, and he drew stick down along the cow and says he:

'Two horns ...'

'Saviour above,' says the widow woman, 'and how many horns do you want to put on my cow. That'll be three already!'

'Why did you speak?' says he. 'I told you not to speak. My whole work's lost and I can't do it twice. You may take your cow away.'

And she had to, but he kept her to her bargain and had a brave life of it while he lived ever after.

86. Rising a Wind Off Rathlin

It was supposed to be a witch that lived on Islay near Scotland. It was supposed to be her took up Raackery in her apron from Armoy glen in Antrim and when she was going home the apron string broke and Raackery fell where it is the day.

There was a Raackery boat in Islay one time, and every morning when they went to leave the seas were wild or the shores bad [surf running] or it was blowing and storming. So this old Islay man says:

'If I was yous I'd club up among yous and give that old woman a few shillings.'

So they had to do it and the sea got as calm as glass. Then they had no wind and had to give her more money. And she give them a woollen thread. There were three knots on it. They were to loose the first one for a breeze and the second one for a wind, but the third was for a storm.

The next morning they set off and loosed a knot and a breeze got up and they got away. They loosed a second knot and the wind riz. When they got a bit further one man says:

'We'll test this old one's strength.'

And they loosed the third knot. That was when they were off the East Lighthouse here off the Island. The wind blew them right past and into Cushendun Bay.

11 TALES ABOUT THE DEVIL

The storytellers: Michael E Morris and his sister Mary

87. The Divil's Own Cow

It was this woman and she sent one of her friends to this Fair to buy a cow for her, and they bought the cow, and when they come with this cow to her she asked who they'd bought her off, and she was told: a Protestant man.

'Aw,' says this woman, 'go in quick one of yous and take me out the bottle of Holy Water till I give her a shake at once and be on the safe side.'

She lived convenient to a bleach green and her man worked at the linen, and had to work constantly, and that's why he couldn't go to the Fair. So this one of her friends run in and takes this bottle from the corner of the dresser and runs out with it. And the woman never looks at the bottle only takes it and shakes it on the cow in the Name of the Father, Son and Holy Ghost - and begod the bleddy cow lept and went mad. Every shake of water that lit on the cow put her worse.

And says the old woman, shaking more and more:

'Aw, but wasn't I right? The Divil himself is deep in her.'

And what the hell was it only a bottle of vitriol that'd be used at the linen. Putting the cow stone mad ...!

88. The Travelling Woman and the Divil

This man and woman weren't long married and the Divil was doing his damndest to put between them and he couldn't. So this day he met a Travelling Woman on the road and they talked, and they made a bargain: the Divil was to give her a new pair of boots if she could put between the man and wife and she said she could.

The Travelling Woman was well known to the man and wife: she'd get a drop of tea and a bed in the corner any night she'd call. So when she went into the house she was made welcome and she asked the woman how was her husband behaving himself.

'The best in the world,' says the woman.

'Is he good to you?'

'Couldn't be better,' she says. 'I can find no fault with him at all. He'll hardly let me do a hand's turn.'

'Well now,' says the Travelling Woman, 'he'd be even better still, and I can put you on a way of going about it. There's two hairs,' says she, 'away down here on his thrapple [lower part of throat]. Some night when you get him sleeping, take his razor and shave them off nice and easy, and you'll find he'll be even a better man to you.'

And what hell did the Travelling Woman do then but, when she seen her chance, she got talking to the husband and asked him how he was pleased with his woman. Oh, she was the best, he sayed.

'I don't know,' says the Travelling Woman; 'I wouldn't trust her. Thon woman you have would cut your throat some night if she got the chance.'

And here, begod, the man sort of believed her; and this night when he was in bed and letting on to be sound asleep he seen his own woman coming up with a razor in her hand and she went to shave the two hairs off his thrapple. He up with his two feet and give it to her in the chest and knocked her kicking on the broad of her back. And the murder and rowing riz between the two of them.

So the Travelling Woman, her job done, met the Divil on the road this day at some appointed place, and he come meeting her with the new boots. But the Divil had them on the end of a pitchfork. And that's the way he reached them till her.

'I wouldn't come nearther than the fork to you,' the Divil says, 'for you're seven times worse than I am myself.'

89. The Lawyer and the Divil

There was this man in it one time and he had three sons and he wanted to make something of them but hadn't the money. So he sells himself to the Divil to rise money to school the three boys, and he did. He made one a priest, the other a doctor and the third one was a lawyer. The Divil give him the money to pay for their education.

But anyway, at the end of seven years the Divil showed up to claim the old man and his soul and take him and it down to Hell. He had his three sons there, or one at a time in with him. So when the Divil come the priest began to pray and beg and appeal for sparings [extension of time] for his father, and in the heel of the hunt he got a few years more off the Divil for his father.

When that was up and the Divil come again the doctor was there and he appealed for sparings for his father and got them. And when the Divil come a third time to claim the old fellow the lawyer was there. The lawyer says to the Divil:

'You've given sparings to my father twice already and I know you can't be expected to do it again. But,' says he, 'as a last request, will you give him sparings while that butt of a candle is there?'

The candle was burning on the table.

The Divil said he would: it was only a butt of a candle and wouldn't be long in it.

At that the lawyer picks up the butt of a candle and blows it out and puts it in his pocket. And that was that! The Divil had to keep to his bargain and go without the old man, for the lawyer held on to the butt of a candle. Trust the lawyer to beat the Divil.

90. Banagher Beats the Divil

Well, if that doesn't beat Banagher ... and sure Banagher beat the Divil. I don't know who in hell Banagher was but he was one smart fellow.

One time Banagher and the Divil were walking along the road this day and there was a field of spuds growing. Banagher says to the Divil:

'What half will be yours?'

'I'll take the tops,' says the Divil.

'Very good,' says Banagher, 'but let them ripen first.'

Well, when the time of year come the Divil had to put up with the stalks and they were all withered of course. So the following year the pair of boys were walking along this road again and there was a field of oats growing.

'Well,' says Banager, 'and what'll your half be this time?'

'Aw-haw,' says the Divil, 'you done me last year. This year you won't do me. You take the tops this year and I'll take the roots.'

So Banagher done the Divil again.

91. 'I Thought You Were the Parish Priest'

There was a *gasun* one time hired with an old crusty parish priest that was death on dancing and any sort of hellery. The servant-boy done wee turns about the house and looked after the parish priest's pony and trap, and he had a bed on a loft in the stable above the pony's head.

But you can't put an old head on young shoulders and youth must have its fling, and of course the servant-boy used to sneak out now and then when he'd hear word of a dance in some house. His only dread was the parish priest while he was away would be called for a sick-call and he wasn't there to yoke the pony in the trap and drive him.

He was out this night at a dance anyway and he heard word that someone was bad, and he flew back to the parochial house for fear it would be the parish priest would be called, and not maybe the curate.

Now there was an old thorn bush on his way back, near the avenue going up the parochial house. Everyone said there was always something not right seen there out of hours and that no one unless they had urgent business should pass it alone at night.

The poor *gasun* of a servant-boy was drowned in his own sweat, not for fear, but for the way he was running. And here coming up to the big old thorn bush in the starlight he sees this black figure standing waiting. He got as weak as water, and he blessed himself. If you do that or speak to something not of this world it has the power to answer you.

'In the Name of God who are you?' he calls out before he could make out who or what the black figure was.

The figure answers back: 'I'm the Divil out of Hell.'

'Aw, thanks be to God,' says the servant-boy. 'I was sure you were the parish priest.'

92. Married to His Sister

Another time this man tore out of the house after a row with the wife. He went along the road going nowhere at all only cursing and damning his soul into hell and out again over the targer of a wife he had. And here he falls in with this strange man who walked out from under a bush along the road where he could have been sheltering.

They got into crack anyway. Passing this house here was another man and wife flailing old hell out of other and calling other for all the wrong names in the wide world.

They stood to listen.

'What's going on in there?' says the strange man, 'or what's in that house?'

'Need you ask?' says our man. 'Can't you see it's the divil outa hell is in that house.'

'Go long,' says the strange man, drawing the back of his hand across the other fellow's jaw in a welt that stumbled him: 'it's you and the likes of you gives me the bad name.'

'Why,' says this man, 'don't tell me you're the Divil himself?'

'I am,' says the Divil, still mad.

The other man put out his hand. 'Leave it there,' says he; 'we're related. For I think I'm married to your sister.'

93. 'Can I Buy a Divil, Da?'

I've heard it said that the women are the divil, for a woman wouldn't be a woman without a bit of a divil in her: it's the real quiet ones you want to watch out for ... they could build a nest in your lug or take the eye out of your head and come back for the eye-lash before you knew what they were up to.

So I never could blame the old mountainy man that put no trust in any woman. He lived at the back of the mountain - and yous know what they're like at the back of the mountain God look to them! - and he had one *gahm* of a son. Maybe he married a bad woman and one was more than enough. He reared the son up himself and never let him out to church or chapel, Mass or market until he was a big hefty lump of a codger maybe well over sixteen.

All the young fellow knew were other old fellows like his father sitting, spitting round the fire at night telling stories of ghosts and divils.

This day anyhow the father seen he had better let the son see a bit of the world, so he took him out as far as Dundalk this Fair Day. They travelled in the ass and cart. Well man alive the first woman the son got his lamps on the eyes stood in his head like a cat a-drowning and he says to his father:

'Da,' says he, 'what's that?'

'That's a Divil,' says the father.

The young fellow had heard enough about the Divil and the Divil's imps to scare the living day-lights out of him. Until he seen another woman and asked the same question.

'What's that, Da?'

'Another divil,' says the father.

And on and on until they reached the town. The father stabled the ass in the back-way and set this *gahm* of a son standing on the footpath. And says he:

'I have markets to make and there's no use trailing you with me. You can walk from here up to that corner and walk back, and that way you won't go astray or get lost till I come back. There's cake-shops with ginger-ale along here, and here's half-a-crown and buy what you like.'

And he went away. How long he was away I don't know, but no man ever run into a town and out with the curse of the place on him and he had a few drinks, met a few people, and didn't starve his *céilí* with them anyway. And when he come back, here was the son standing like a statue and he could see he hadn't budged an inch. And he still had the half-crown tight in his fist.

'My God,' says the father, 'did you not move at all? And did you not buy nothing?'

'No, Da,' says the son.

'And do you not want to buy nothing?'

'I do, Da,' says he. 'Can I buy a divil, Da?'

94. Willy the Wisp

This man he was a blacksmith and he was a very heavy drinker, and no matter how much money he could make he could never get enough to do him. So someone told him that if he'd go out to such'n a place, in the middle of the night, and call Old Nick three times Nick'd appear to him, and give him as much money as he'd want.

So begod he'd do anything for money; so he went out to this place in the middle of the night and called three times to Old Nick, and the Divil appeared to him: and he give him as much money as he'd spend for seven years; but he'd have to come and take him when the time would be up.

Well begod anyway, he was a blacksmith, and he had piles of money: he had so much money he was drinking away, and he was building a town; he joined [began] to build a town in the County Meath, and the town he built was Trim.

He was building this town and he still had the forge; and this saint appeared to him; and he helped him; and he says to the blacksmith:

'I'll give you three wishes, and whatever you wish for you'll get it.'

'Well,' he says, 'the first wish I want, any man that takes my hammer in his hand he cannot get rid of it till I take it from him.

'And the second wish is,' he says, 'that anyone that sits in my armchair he'll never get out of it till I take him out of it.

'And the third wish,' he says, 'any money that goes into my purse will never come out till I take it out of it.'

'Ah ... if only you had wished for Heaven and you'd get it,' says the saint.

But anyway, he was working away at the town, and in the forge, and he was shoeing a horse, and the seven years was up and the Divil come for him. And Willy - that was his name - was in the forge, working in the forge, when the Divil come.

'Come ...'

'Right,' says Willy; 'take that hammer and time this shoe with a few taps.'

The Divil took the hammer.

'When I shoe this mare I'll be with you,' says Willy.

The Divil took the hammer, and Willy left him and went up to his house and left him there hammering in the forge for three days, and when Willy came back the Divil was hammering away. And the Divil begged him for all sakes and as much more money to release him for another seven years.

'Right,' says Willy; 'give me that hammer.'

And away with the Divil.

So Willy had piles of money for another seven years.

Still working away in his forge, and the seven more years was up and the Divil come for him. And Willy was working in the forge again.

'Are you ready for to come the day? You must come the day,' says the Divil.

'Right,' says Willy; 'I'll be with you when I get a cup of tea. Come up to the house,' he says, 'and when I have a cup of tea I'll be with you. Sit down in that chair.'

Got the cup of tea. The Divil sat down. So Willy left him in the armchair, and Willy went down to the forge and reddened an iron, and come up and started to persecute the Divil.

The Divil begged him for all sakes to let him free and he'd give him as much more money for another seven years; but he'd surely have to come then.

'Right,' says Willy; 'come on; get out.'

And the Divil went; and Willy carried on for another seven years more. And the Divil come in the latter end and Willy was once more working in the forge.

'Are you coming? ... You have to come.'

'Right,' says Willy. 'I'll be with you.'

Of course all his money was gone and the time was up, seven years, he would get no more. So Willy threw his coat on his shoulder and walked off with the Divil and was just going by a public-house.

'I'm very dry,' says Willy; 'I'd like a drink. I have no money,' he says. 'You could turn yourself into a half-crown,' he says, 'and put it in my purse, and you'd be out of the public-house as soon as me.'

So, all right, the Divil did it. Willy put the half-crown into his purse and went back to the forge. He lit the fire, and he put the purse into the fire and reddened the purse and the half-crown in it, and he put it on the anvil and joined to hammer it with the sledge.

The Divil yelled to be let go. He says:

'Let me go,' he says, 'and I'll give you as much more money and never ask you to come with me.'

'Right,' says Willy.

So he did, and the Divil was free; and Willie worked away. And when Willy died he went to Heaven. He was met at the gates.

'Aw, you can't come in here. You sold yourself to the Divil. You'll have to go below.'

He went down below to Hell and the Divil wouldn't let

him in there either: he was afraid if Willy got in he'd lay Hell waste. So he lit a wisp in the fire and he give to Willy and sent him back. And he's going from Heaven to Hell to this day, and that's what they call 'Willy The Wisp'.

12 THE SAINTS

The storytellers: James Loughran

95. Columbcille Curses the Rushes

The soldiers were after Columbcille this time, and he had to make off in a hurry, and he had time only to get one boot on him, or one boot tied. And he had to make off and run through a field of rushes and he lost the boot and the rushes jagged his feet.

And he cursed the rushes: 'For a green top never to be on them again.' And if you remark it there isn't to this day; and if you open the old rush and find a new rush inside, the young rush has a brown top too.

96. The Woman's Graveyard in Carrickmore [Co Tyrone]

It's to the fore to this very day outside of Carrickmore here in the County Tyrone and they call it: Relig na mBan, The Woman's Graveyard and Columbcille done that. No dead man and no living woman dare go into it, and I'll tell you how all that happened.

It was Columbcille; he was here at Carrickmore and he had a wee chapel here one time too. He was coming down the road this day, in the morning, and he met in with one of these unfortunate girls that never was married and she had a youngster in her arms, it seems they were as common even then as pins and needles and bootlaces. Coming down the road Columbcille met her near the chapel and he bid her good morning and then he says:

'What do you call the child?'

'Columbcille,' says she.

Well, he called his men then to ring the Jow-jeelta - that was his bell that they used to swear on here ... It'd ring if you told a lie. He called them to ring the bell and they rung the bell and he told her to walk on. And he told her to keep walking till she couldn't hear the bell ringing no longer. And she got as far from Carrickmore to that graveyard. And then she dropped dead and they buried her there. And it's only women were ever buried there since.

Canon Carr and Father Donnelly brought Cardinal Logue here to me to answer that and I told the story as I've told you and Cardinal Logue said he couldn't see it and what did it mean. So I told him. For if Columbcille let her away, what was to stop her saying the child was his when its name was the same as his.

'That's right, that's right,' says Cardinal Logue.

97. Columbcille's Bullock

The time Columbcille was building his church here at Carrickmore in this part of Tyrone he had a great bullock, a powerful bullock. It kept him and the men he had working at the building of the chapel in meat. Every night when they'd have done they would kill the bullock and ate it, and they used blood then to mix with the mortar, and in the morning the bullock would be out grazing as good as ever.

Columbcille warned them that they weren't to meddle with the marrow in the shin bones of this bullock and that was all. Anything bar that and the bullock would be as good as ever.

But this night ... Was it McMahon or Loughran now was in it? ... I forget. Whoever it was says he:

'I'll try the marrow and see what happens.'

And he took a sledge and broke one of the shin bones of the bullock when it was killed and he had that; and in the morning the bullock was as good as ever, only it was lame in one of its front legs.

And that angered Columbcille, and he cursed the man that done it: and he said that three of them would be killed before the building was over. Two of them was killed when the walls fell on them, and there's a third yet to be killed, and it wouldn't be safe to stand with him agin any wall.

98. Columbcille and the End of the World

There's a miller to be called Peter Dick and he'll have two heels on the one foot. Columbcille prophesised that. That'll be the end. Columbcille dreamed all his prophecies: so the old people used to say.

13 RELIGIOUS TALES

The storytellers: Rosie Emerson

99. St Peter and Christ and the Miser

St Peter and Our Lord were going along this day, talking away to other, and they met this beggar. St Peter put his hand in his pocket and he give the beggar some coin. Our Lord didn't say a haet, kept walking on, saying nothing. So a bit further on they met in with another beggar looking for help. And St Peter reached this man two coins.

They walked on a piece and Our Lord says to St Peter:

'How does it come you give the first man one coin and you give two coins to the second man?'

'Well,' says St Peter, 'I'll soon tell You that. That first man we met didn't really want it,' says St Peter, 'but that second man was sorely in need of it.'

'Aye?' says Our Lord. And says Our Lord then:

'If you go back along the road you'll get that second man dead now,' says Our Lord; 'he dropped out of his standing.'

So St Peter went back along the road and he got the second beggarman lying dead. So he looked in the dead man's pockets and he got fifty or a hundred-and-fifty [money] ... I can't be sure of the number now. But anyway St Peter took twenty and left the rest.

He come back to where Our Lord was standing.

'You were right,' says St Peter. 'I got him lying dead.'

'And what did you do?' says Our Lord

'I went through his pockets and took twenty,' says St Peter.

'What did you do that for?' asks Our Lord.

'Oh, some poor man will stand in need of it,' he says.

'You needn't then,' says Our Lord. 'Throw them coins all away. For the miser's penny is no good for nobody.'

100. The Penitent Thief

St Joseph and the Virgin and the Child Jesus were on the Flight into Egypt to escape the wrath of Herod at the Slaying of the Innocents.

They had little food and less water and habitations were scarce. At length they came to a poor house where the Virgin asked for milk or food for the Child Jesus. The woman of the house, with a big family of her own, said she had no food for her own family. The infant in the family, about the same age as the Child Jesus, was bawling with hunger. Just the same the woman of the house noticed something strange and unusually bright about the Child the Virgin carried in her arms.

The Virgin told the woman to put on a pot and fill it with stones. The woman did as she was told. The pot came to the boil and the Virgin told the woman to take it off: she did so and found that the stones had turned into potatoes.

The Virgin then asked for water to wash the Child Jesus. Water was scarce; but the woman of the house put some in a basin. The Virgin washed the Child Jesus, and then the woman of the house washed her own child in the same water.

Her infant, because of the grace of that washing in the same water, was the Penitent Thief on Calvary on one side of Christ when He was crucified.

101a. Christ Explains Why Fishermen Drown

St Peter, being a fisherman, was particularly anxious during a storm. He later learned that a vessel he knew had been lost with all hands. He said they were good men; and he asked Christ why God should allow such a disaster to happen.

Christ replied that they had been lost because there was one sinner among them. This reply puzzled and depressed St Peter even more so, and he walked behind Christ, deep in thought.

It was a hot day and they were walking in the shade of trees. Absently-mindedly, deep in depression, St Peter accidently disturbed a wasps' nest hanging from a branch. The insects swarmed madly around St Peter and he tried to beat them off. One returned and stung him. St Peter got so mad he destroyed the nest entirely.

Then Christ pointed out to him that that was why God had allowed the fishing vessel to founder.

101b.

A Roman Catholic man who neglects to observe the obligation of attending Mass on Sundays and Holy Days is being unbraided by a new priest for his neglect, and is asked to give his reason for doing so.

He says that if anything is stolen during Mass no one can blame him!

102. Why the Tinker Keeps Travelling

Before the Crucifixion of Christ no blacksmith could be found who would consent to make the nails. But a tinker agreed to do so.

Hence, from that day to this the tinker is condemned to wander the roads of the world for his livelihood.

103. Christ

Christ was red-haired: and He was the only man in the world who was ever exactly six feet tall, neither more nor less.

104. Judas

Judas hanged himself on the bole-tree bush [elder].

And the Cross on which Christ was crucified was made out of the bole-tree bush; and that's why from that day to this you never see six feet of it straight.

14 PADDY THE IRISHMAN

The storytellers: Mickey McCuaig

105. 'Bags of Heat and Bags of Help'

Pat and Mick died and one went to Heaven and the other to Hell. The fellow in Hell one day shouts up to Pat:

'What sort of a time have you up there?'

Pat replied:

'Not what it was cracked up to be at all. It's my job to hang out the stars and push out the moon at night, and to take them in in the morning; and I'm foundered with the cold, and there's no help. How's things with you down there?'

Mick answered:

'Bags of heat and bags of help.'

106. Sentenced to be Hanged

The Englishman and the Scotsman and the Irishman had been sentenced together to be hanged, but were give the choice of tree from which they were to hang.

The Englishman said he wished to be hanged from the Old Oak of England: the Scotsman said he wished to hang from a Scots fir. Paddy said he wished to hang from a gooseberry bush.

The judge interposed to remind him that a gooseberry bush was neither strong enough nor tall enough to hang him.

Paddy replied:

'I'll wait till it grows, your honour.'

107. The Pope's Luggage

The Englishman and the Scotsman and the Irishman died together, and all three presented themselves at the Gates of Heaven. St Peter refused admission to them except - on the intervention of St Patrick [who is said to judge the Irish on The Last Day] - to Paddy: Paddy refused to enter without his two companions, so all three were excluded.

A Pope died at the time. He arrived at the Gates of Heaven and was welcomed with open arms.

Then Paddy told the Scotsman to get up on his back; he did so. He told the Englishman to get up then on the Scotsman's back, which he did. Paddy told them to keep their heads down.

He went up to the Gates and shook them. St Peter appeared, opened them and asked who was there.

Paddy called out:

'The Pope's luggage.'

They were admitted.

108. You Want to Change Your Religion

With a straw rope on its leg Paddy drove his pig on to a boat bound for Liverpool where the market was better.

Driving the pig off the boat and into the streets of Liverpool the pig got wildly upset by the noise of the horse-drawn drays on the cobbles. There was a Protestant church near by and the gate was open. The pig broke away from Paddy and dashed through the gate. He pursued it with his cap in his hand, recovered the pig and began to lash it.

He says:

'Bad luck to your soul, you're not ten minutes in the country and you want to change your religion.'

109. The Flea's Wake

In England for the first time Paddy was looking for lodgings.

He had heard fearsome stories about the fleas in English rooms; so he asked his landlady if there were any in the room he had taken. He asked her to be honest about it. She confessed that there might be one.

At breakfast next morning he said he had good news for her.

'That flea of yours is dead,' he announced.

She said she was glad but was he sure.

'I'm certain sure,' says Paddy; 'for all the fleas in the street were up there at his wake last night.'

110. The Bear's Den

Pat and Mick walking a foreign country came on a bear's den; the cubs were playing outside and ran in as they approached. Pat said:

'Them's powerful great pups. We'll get one and take it home.'

Pat crept into the den to seize one of the cubs when the

old bear returned. As it was going in to the den Mick, concealed outside, seized it by the tail. From inside Pat called out:

'What's blocking the light?'

Mick replied:

'If this bleddy tail breaks you'll soon know what's blocking the light.'

111a. Paddy at Sea

A seaman got a job as fireman for his brother. A storm arose and the ship began to founder. The captain cried for the crew to take to the boats.

The seamen hurried to the deck-grid above the stoke-hold where his brother was firing the furnace and cried out for him to get up, that the ship was sinking. The brother below called up:

'Let her sink to hell: she's none of ours.'

111b.

After their ship had foundered two seamen were on a raft. They were being swamped. One asked the other if he could pray. He replied it was years since he had done so but would do his best. He began:

'Man above, it's ages since either of us have bothered You; but if You get us safe out of this it'll be as long again.'

15 FANTASTIC TALES

The storytellers: Francis McBride

112. His Westcoat Barked

John McLoughlin that lived out The Point [Warrenpoint] road had this hound. There never was the beating of her ... sure she pupped in a teapot.

One time she was carrying pups and a hare riz and she made after it and ripped the belly out of herself on barbed wire on this ditch and the greyhound pups spilled out of her. And one of them up like hell and after the hare and stuck till the hare till he caught it and killed it.

And when the greyhound was dead John McLoughlin had her skinned and he put a back in a westcoat [waistcoat] with her skin. And one day he out over the water in Omeath hunting and this hare riz and begod John said the back of the westcoat on him ... barked!

113. A Brave Good Shot

Wiley used to tell the crack and would swear on any book it was true. He was out poaching and it was one of them old guns you loaded with a ram-rod, a muzzle-loader. He was loading the gun after a shot when what does he see crossing the neck of the hill but a flock of wild geese. They were nice and low flying south. He was that excited seeing the wild geese so low and so handy that he ups with the gun and fires before he thought of taking the ram-rod out of the barrel.

Well! The shot of the gun with the ram-rod in it give such a kick that it sent Wiley flying back on his arse into the heart of a whin-bush, and what does he land on but a big Scotch hare asleep in its den in the whin-bush and he killed it with his fall without as much as a squeal. When he gathered himself out of the whin-bush and took the hare with him, here above the Owenkillew River he seen these two wild geese come fluttering down and them pinned together ... with the ram-rod out of the gun: right through them and sticking out the far side. Down they come and flopped into the water near the bridge. And when he went to get them he found that the end of the ram-rod had speared a salmon on the redd in the river. Now that's what I call a brave good shot ...!

114. A Bush Grew Out of His Back

There used to be an old flat ferry at Narrow Water: ones going with cattle and sheep and horses from the far side to the Fair at Warrenpoint would cross that way: I mind it well meself.

This man anyway had a horse with him ... he was taking it from summer grazing somewhere ... and whatever hell happened, the horse slipped or jumped over and broke its back in two. He runs at once and cuts a bucky briar and run it up the horse's backside and it joined the two parts of the back and he took the horse home. And this tree grew out of the briar in its back and grew up and up and up. And this day in the springtime in the field he says:

'I wonder what's up there?'

So he gets up on the horse's back and climbs the tree and found a lovely country at the top and it full of seed oats. So he shook the bush and the seed oats fell down and into the ground and he had a lovely crop of oats. But coming down he slipped and landed into this rock and stuck in it like cement. And this hure of a fox come and started to pish on him. The only thing he could get his hand to was an old rusty blade of a scythe and he fired that at the fox and it caught in the fox's tail and he went mad round the field and didn't quit till he'd cut every grain of the oats.

16 TALES OF ANIMALS, BIRDS AND INSECTS

The storytellers: Myles Dolan

115. The Cat and the Mouse in a Public House

A mouse pursued by a cat in a public house fell into an open barrel of whiskey. The mouse cried to the cat to be taken out of the barrel. To which the cat answered that he would only have to eat the mouse. The mouse replied:

'I don't care: anything bar to die in drink.'

The cat pawed the mouse out of the barrel, set it down, and then began to play with the mouse, which at last was able to run and escape into a hole. The cat said:

'You made a bargain that if I'd take you out of the barrel of whiskey you'd let me eat you.'

The mouse answered:

'Who gives any heed to what a fella says in drink?'

116. A Clever Fox

The fox was the Danes' dogs, just as the weasels were their cats and there's tales about them too. This is only one about a fox.

There was a man one time lived up the Slie' Gullion mountain road and he was bothered with the fox taking his hens. In the latter end to beat the fox he took the fowl into the kitchen and put them roosting on the rungs under the table, and when he had them trained he cut a wee square hole in the door for the hens to go in and out of when he wasn't around. It was a thatched house with an open fire on the hearth.

This day he was in Newry and he put the hens in the kitchen before he was leaving, and put on a good fire of turf and smothered it with *greesha* to keep it lit till he'd get back. He bought a new pair of boots in Newry, made his markets and come home. And when he got home and into the house there was the thief of a fox in the kitchen with one hen dead and in his mouth. The fox had seen him go off and had delused he'd be away a long time and had squeezed himself through the hole in the door and into the kitchen.

The man grabbed a cutty spade he had behind the door for closing it at night and says to himself:

'Now I have him. For he can't get through the hole in the door quick enough until I give him a good crig of the spade.'

And he makes for the fox with the spade, closing the door first of all. He dropped the boots to take up the spade and the fox run and hid under the table. He got him out of that but the fox run and hid somewhere else below the dresser. He got him out of that and round and round the house they went and he was sure he had the fox done for and cornered.

But what did the fox do? Running round the house past the door this time he snapped up one of the new boots the man had bought and run on with it in his mouth and passing the hearth-stone he heaved it out of his mouth into the fire and it started to burn.

The man let a shout and run to save the new boot and while he was doing that the fox had time to squeeze back out through the hole in the door and away.

117. The Last Fox on Rathlin Island

I heard it told on the Island that the last fox in Ireland - or the one on Rathlin - was drowned by a limpet on the shore. The fox come along and went to lick the limpet and it closed its shell on him and held him by the tongue till the tide came in and drowned him.

118. The Cat and the Fox

The fox met the cat one day and they got arguing and says the fox:

'Poor puss. I have ten tricks but you have only one.'

Just then the hounds were heard coming in the distance and the fox made off. He run this way and that way and every other way and in the latter end he was caught and killed.

But what happened the cat: he had only the one trick. When the hounds come the cat run up a tree and was safe.

119. The Fox Rids Himself of Fleas

To rid itself of fleas: Gets a ewe's tail and holds it in he's mouth. Immerses itself slowly in a well, tail first: the fleas jump up the body ahead of the encroaching water until finally all collected into the ewe's tail. Fox pushes the tail off and gets out of the well.

120. The Ass and the Bullock

It was the time that animals could talk, and this man owned an ass and a bullock: the bullock used to do all the ploughing and the ass done nothing only a bit of light carting; kicking up his heels most of the time.

Anyway, the bullock thought he was getting too much of it while the ass done nothing; and when the bullock would come in at night to the stable where they were both housed the ass would laugh and caa-hee at the bullock the way he was groaning and moaning with the tiredness ploughing the live-long day.

So the bullock got fed up and hit on a plan. He let on to be sick. When the farmer put in his armful of hay and a mash at night he never left a mouth on either. Nor never lipped it the next night.

So the farmer goes and says to his wife:

'The bullock's bad and I can't work him. I'll have to take the ass out the morra and plough with him instead.'

So the ass was taken out the next morning and ploughed all day, and when he come in that night he was hardly fit to move ... No caa-heeing and laughing out of him now. It was the bullock was doing all the laughing.

The next day the ass was taken out again and come in that night more done out than ever. Says the bullock to him:

'How do you like the ploughing now?'

'Ah,' says the ass, 'I'll get used to it in time if I have days to live, but your days are numbered.'

'How do you make that out?' says the bullock.

'Well,' says the ass ... Stupid as an ass ... They couldn't have been that stupid ... 'I heard the farmer tell the woman the day that seeing you were still sick the sooner they got the butcher to you the better. "Better get something," says he, "instead of having to bury him." '

When the bullock heard that he started in to ate the hay and didn't leave a grain of it in the manger, nor a taste of the mash, and when the farmer come in in the morning and seen he'd cleared up everything he said he be to be fit and well again and took him out to the ploughing and the ass was left to kick up his heels as before.

121. The Talking Jackdaw

They used to say that if you split a jackdaw's tongue with a silver sixpence or thrupenny bit it could learn to talk.

This jackdaw could talk anyway, but the fellow that had it died or went away and the jackdaw flew off and went with its own kind.

And this day this fellow was ploughing in a field with a forth in it: a plough-man hired for wages and he was new to the country. And what the hell got behind him among the other birds and crows only this jackdaw. And this time when it saw a great big worm it says:

'Gobble him up.'

The ploughman looked at the forth and seen no one and got sort of afeared. Then the jackdaw seen another big worm and says:

'Gobble him now.'

At that the ploughman left plough and horses and harness and away home like hell and said he was quitting.

'Why,' says his master, 'what's wrong?'

His master was a minister who'd just been moved into that part of the world too.

'There's something not right in that field,' says the ploughman. 'I won't stand in it again.' Telling the minister what had happened, about the voice saying: 'Gobble him up.'

The minister said he was talking nonsense, that he'd only imagined it, and that he'd go back to the field with him and walk around for a few scores. So he did and the ploughing started again and the minister was walking beside the ploughman, and the jackdaw lit at their heels; and this time he sees two big worms.

'Gobble the both of them,' says he.

And minister and ploughman took to their heels away to hell altogether.

122. The Smith and his Ass

Jemmy Ryan was one day hurrying home from Dundalk to shoe wheels in Ballymascanlon, and he was flaking hell out of the ass. And who was coming behind him only Canon Donnellan, and when he could stick it no longer he says to Jemmy Ryan:

'Don't you know that that's the animal Our Lord rode through Jerusalem?'

'It wasn't this one,' says Jemmy, 'or He'd never go through it.'

123. The Weasel's Spit

We have two kinds of weasels in Ireland. The thing we call a weasel the day is only a stoat: the real Irish weasel they said was as big as a cat. The Danes took them in here for their cats.

I never saw a dead weasel nor no other white man: for they bury their dead. They're not a right nor proper thing to interfere with. Now Paddy McDermott one time in Annaverna was mowing hay. And he come on this weasel's nest, in the ground, and three or four young ones in it. What did he do ...? He lifted a wee cock of hay ... didn't kill them or anything ... and put the hay on top of them in the nest.

There come a can of milk for a drink to the field and it was left on the head-rig. And when Paddy looked, here he sees the old weasel and she was trying to find the nest. Next thing Paddy sees is another weasel on the head-rig, and it had the lid off the can and it spat into the milk.

When Paddy seen that he run and lifted the wee cock of hay off the weasel's nest and mowed on for a while. And then begod if the old weasel wasn't on the head-rig again and doing her damndest to push over the can of milk, cowp it!

If Paddy McDermott had as much as taken one sip of that milk it would have poisoned him stone dead after the weasel spitting in it. And she knew that and wanted to destroy it ... Because he uncovered the nest again.

124. Why the Ass Has a Cross on Its Back

The ass has a cross on its back for a purpose: it carried Our Lord and He left the cross that way so that He'd be known.

125. The Hedgehog Races the Hare

Did you ever know the way the hedgehog won the bet from the hare?

They were to run a race and the hedgehog said he would win. So the hare took him on. The race took place in priddy-drills, a drill that was moulded, after being riz.

And there was one hedgehog at the top of this drill and another at the bottom. So when the hare would run to the top he'd see a hedgehog before him, and when he'd get to the bottom the hedgehog was there before him; he didn't know there was two in it.

'Up and at it,' says the hedgehog to the hare.

Between them anyway they killed the hare [by exhaustion].

126. The Robin

The Robin has a red-breast for the same thing. When Our Lord was hanging on the Cross the blood was dropping on the ground, and the Robin was carrying the leaves and putting them on the blood, and this other bird was carrying them away, and as fast as this other bird would carry them away the Robin would carry them back; and that's how it got its breast red with the blood. The other bird could be the Jinny-Wren. I'm not sure.

127. The Wren

Did you ever hear how the Jinny-Wren come to be left making its nest in a wee hole in the ditch? Well, I'll tell you. At the beginning of time the birds could talk and it was for which of them could fly the highest. It was The Lord God said it had to be done ... Who else!

Well, all the birds began to fly and the Jinny-Wren was the smallest; she was that small she lit on the eagle's back, and she was that light the eagle never noticed. The eagle can fly the highest of any bird: but the Jinny-Wren said she went higher. And for doing what she done God took the power off her and put her hoking for a nest in the ditch with only a wee hole to go into. And that's why the Jinny-Wren can't fly high to this day.

128. 'Don't Forget Yesterday'

One time it seems Our Lord was escaping from the Roman

soldiers, and they were coming very tight [close] on Him and He didn't seem to have much chance of escaping.

So there was a man sowing corn in this field, and He asked the man if he would help Him to escape. The man said he would but didn't know how.

'It's very simple,' said Our Lord. 'When the soldiers pass here and ask if you've seen Me I want you to say that you did see Me. Don't tell a lie. Say I passed when you were sowing corn.'

So the man said he would; and when the soldiers came up and asked if he had seen Our Lord he said he had, and that He had passed when he was sowing the field of corn.

But now the corn had shot up and was as ripe as ever it would be, and the soldiers says:

'Oh well, if He passed when you were sowing it where must He be by now when it's ripe it is.'

And it was then that the Dhool [black beetle] spoke up: 'He passed here yesterday. He passed here yesterday.'

So that's why the old people would say you should always put your foot on a Dhool and kill it dead. They'd do that and say in Irish: 'Remember yesterday' or 'Don't forget yesterday.'

129. Why a Dog's Nose is Always Cold

There was a leak come in The Ark the time Noah was out in it in the flood, and it would have sunk, only the dog put his nose in the leak and that stopped it. The warmest day in summer and a dog's nose would be freezing cold ever since.

130. Three Coldest Things in the World

A frog.
A dog's nose.
A woman's elbow.

17 THE DANES

The storytellers: FrankMcAuley

131. The Danes Could Make Wine from Heather

The Danes could make wine out of the heather but they took the secret with them. For when there was only two Danes left alive in Ireland after the battle and all the rest of them killed, the Irish said they had to find out how to make wine out of the heather. These two Danes were father and son. Says the father to them:

'Kill my son and I'll tell you, for if you let him live he'll only tell on me.'

So they killed the son. And then the father says:

'Now yous can kill me, for I'll never tell.'

And they killed him on the spot.

132. A Wild Bad Day on the Braes of Layde

The Danes owned all Ireland one time. One time a man from Cushendall, a sea captain, was in the Danes' country for spars and got talking to this old Dane. He told him where he come from, County Antrim.

'What part?' says the Dane.

He told him: Cushendall.

'Man,' says the old Dane, 'this will be a wild bad day on the Braes of Layde.' Layde a townland above Cushendall. 'Many a time I lay up there,' says the old Dane.

133a. The Danes Own All Ireland

To this very day every old Dane leaves his part of Ireland to his sons, and they know where the treasure is buried here and all.

John Kane proved that to be true. He was a butcher as well, and how he got to be in the Danes' country I forget, but he was at sea for a while. He fell in with this old Dane anyway and he took John home with him. There was an old Dane in bed and he was one-hundred-and-four years of age.

'Are you an Irishman?' says the old Dane.

John Kane sayed he was.

'What part of Ireland do you come from?'

He told him: from Ballintoy.

'What part of Ballintoy?'

John Kane told him: he knew all Ballintoy. The old Dane says:

'Do you know such and such'n a farm. Well, that was mine one time. If you go to a certain hill on that farm of land,' he says and he named the hill, 'there's a grey stone ... it rings like a bell when you strike it.' ... John Kane knew the stone well ... 'There's a certain well,' says the old Dane. 'Is there not a well above the house?'

There was a well above the house; John Kane knew it well.

'And is there not a sally bush at it?'

John Kane said there was.

'If you hoke there,' says the old Dane, 'you'll get as much gold as would buy out Ballintoy.'

They say that's how John Kane got all the money, the old Dane's money that he hoked up.

134. A Prayer Before Going to Bed

The peace of Our Lord
And the virtue of His Sacred Passion;
The Sign of the Holy Cross,
The purity and the humility
of the Blessed Virgin Mary;
The protection of the Angels
And of all the Elect
Be with me now and at the hour of my death
Sweet Jesus. Amen.

THE STORYTELLERS*

The storytellers : Patrick McCullagh

* For numbers within round brackets, see below, p 156.

Mickey Joe Anderson

Aged 67 in 1955. Farmer and fisherman. Ballygeel, Rathlin, Co Antrim. A man with many traditions about the island and its people and who was looked upon as a traditional arbiter in crises or disputes.

Tale No 73.

Peadar Barry

Aged 58 in 1957. Farmer. Corrags, Clonallon Parish. Never robust in health, Peadar was nevertheless an active local Councillor, associated with the Down Gaelic Athletic Association and eager to promote all kinds of traditional activities. He heard his folk stories from an old neighbour named Barney McNulty.

Tale No 50.

Frank Craig

Aged 64 in 1955. Ballykeel, Rathlin, Co Antrim. Farmer and fisherman. One of the last of the native Gaelic speakers on the island. He had much historical lore and traditions about Rathlin.

Tale No 83.

Neil Craig

Aged 75 in 1955. Caravanalley, Rathlin, Co Antrim. Farmer. One of the last of the Rathlin native speakers of Gaelic.

Tale No 86.

Pat Crangle

Aged about 80 in 1950. Blacksmith. Raholp, Co Down.

Tales Nos 32, (102).

Myles Dolan

Aged 65 in 1974. Farmer. Stranamorth, Dubally Parish, Co Cavan. A good storyteller with much general tradition of the area.

Tales Nos 46, 65, 82, 94.

Tom Dunne

Aged 70 in 1943. Farmer. Dromintee, Dromintee Parish, Co Armagh. A fine storyteller. Heard many of his tales with Breen 'Buck' Murphy and from tramps and beggarwomen who used to stay in his house in his young days.

Tales Nos 69, (115).

Stephen Fitzpatrick

('Stephen the Catholic'.) Aged 70 in 1945. Farmer. Stang, Clonduff Parish, Co Down. Inherited his nickname from his father who was famous locally for his readiness to take part in religious disputations. Stephen was one of the storytellers who adamantly refused to be photographed because, as I learned later, 'his likeness' could be used in some rite of evil witchcraft.

Tales Nos 13, 59A.

Johnny Kelly

Aged 91 in 1954. Farmer and fisherman. Coolngrock, Rathlin Island, Co Antrim. A native of the Ballintoy area on the mainland, he heard his stories there. Had been in Rathlin since before 1900.

Tales Nos 61, 85.

James Loughran

Aged 75 in 1962. Farmer and beetling mill and bleach green worker. Annaverna, Jonesboro Parish, Co Armagh. An able storyteller. He claimed to have forgotten many tales and once said: 'Sure God bless you I heard hundreds on top of hundreds and I forget most of them. You have only a small part of what I heard here in my time with the old fellows. It's a helluva long time ago now.'

Tales Nos 3, 8, 9, 10, 38, 39, 40, 41, 42, 45, 49, 51, 57, 63, 66, 81, 87, 90, 95, 99, 118, 122, 123, 125, 126, 127.

Annie Lynch

Aged 75 in 1963. Widow. Dundalk, Co Louth. A native of the town of Louth area, had worked mainly as a servant-girl and house-keeper in public houses. A woman with a wide knowledge of the traditions of the areas she had lived and worked in, and who loved to talk about this lore.

Tale No 52.

Frank McAuley

Aged 49 in 1952. Farmer. Layde, Cushendall, Co Antrim. A man with a wide knowledge of the history and folklore of the Glens district and associated with Gaelic cultural activities in his area.

Tales Nos (131), (132), (133).

Francis McBride

Aged 60 in 1950. Farmer. Teebane East. Greencastle Parish, Co Tyrone. Always eager and ready to assist in introducing me to storytellers. His own knowledge of local tradition extensive. A man with an impish sense of humour. Had many idiomatic sayings and proverbs.

Tales Nos (18), 113.

James McCann

('Posty'.) Aged 83 in 1942. Farmer and seaman. Dromintee, Dromintee Parish, Co Armagh. Inherited his nickname from his father who had 'carried the post' on foot from Newry to Dromintee. Had many tales from a local Gaelic speaking storyteller named Breen ('Buck') Murphy, later fatally injured by a train in the area on the Belfast-Dublin line. At the end of each tale Breen Murphy used to say: 'And may God leave the priest's share in me. He meant that he hoped to have a priest administer the Last Rites before he died. A priest reached him in time.

Tale No 11.

Micky McCuaig

Aged 60 in 1955. Ballinard, Rathlin, Co Antrim. Farmer and fisherman.

Tale No 75.

Patrick McCullagh

('Padraig Feilimí Láidir'.) Aged 70 in 1950. Farmer and blacksmith and skilled craftsman in rush and woodwork. Curraghinalt, Rousky Parish, Co Tyrone. A speaker of native Gaelic who recorded material for Radio Eireann and the BBC. Specimens of his crafts are in the National Museum. See furthermore my article, 'The Late Patrick McCullagh of Currinalt, Co Tyrone' in *Ulster Folklife* 7 (1961), p 33 - 36.

Tale No (37A-B).

Rose McCurdy

Aged 83 in 1954. Widow. Ballinard, Rathlin, Co Antrim. She had much tradition both of Rathlin and her native Glenshesk on the mainland. She was the first on Rathlin to welcome me with the greeting: 'I always like to meet people from Ireland.'

Tale No 72.

Phill McDonnell

Aged 63 in 1972. Farmer. Moneygashel, Killinagh Parish, Co Cavan. A fine storyteller with much general tradition. Singer and traditional musician on the tin whistle. Claims to have the gifts of fortune-telling and hypnotism.

Tales Nos 26, 71.

Michael E Morris

Aged 55 in 1950. Farmer. Has worked as counter-hand in London and New York. Carnanrancy, Greencastle Parish, Co Tyrone. One of the last of the surviving Gaelic speakers in the area. Very interested in all kinds of traditional activities and has an inimitable folk knowledge of the entire district in Tyrone.

Tales Nos (25), 64, 89, 101A -B.

Mary Murphy

Aged 66 in 1942. My mother. Housewife. Dromintee, Dromintee Parish, Co Armagh. I heard my first folktales from my mother and father in Liverpool, where I was born in 1913. Her father, John Campbell of Ballinamaddy, Dromintee Parish, a small farmer and country carpenter and a noted storyteller.

Tales Nos (103), (104), (124), (128).

Michael Murphy

('Micky Buck') Aged 69 in 1942. My father. Pedlar and seaman, Dromintee, Dromintee Parish, Co Armagh. Heard most of his tales from his uncle and from his grandfather, William Jordan of Tifferum, Dromintee; William Jordan was a Gaelic scribe and minor poet.

Tales Nos (1), 4, 5, (6), (14), (17), (21), 23, (24), (47), (91), (93), (106), (107), (109), (110), (111A - B).

Michael J Murphy

Full time collector. The compiler of this book. Born 1913.

Tales Nos 1, 2, 5, 6, 12, 14, 17, 18, 19, 20, 21, 24, 25, 27, 30, 33A - C, 35, 37A - B, 43, 47, 48, 53, 54, 58, 59B, 60A - B, 67, 70, 74, 77, 78, 79, 80, 84, 91, 92, 93, 100, 102, 103, 104, 105, 106, 107, 108, 109, 110, 111A - B, 115, 116, 117, 119, 120, 121, 124, 128, 130, 131, 132, 133.

Tommy Nugent

Aged 80 in 1951. Farmer. Carrickmore, Co Tyrone.

Tales Nos 96, 97.

Dan Rooney

Aged 78 in 1960. Farmer and carter. Clonallon Parish, Co Down. An able storyteller. At his funeral to Burren cemetery someone in the cortege remarked: 'If things were ever getting too solemn old Dan could always say something that would lift anyone's heart.'

Tales Nos 7, (19), 28, 29, 31, 34, 36, 44, 55, 62, 88, 98, 112, 114, 129.

Michael Rooney

Aged 74 in 1974. Retired County Council worker and farm labourer. Blacklion, Killinagh Parish, Co Cavan. An able storyteller who has much general tradition also. Continually expresses delight that interest is being taken in the folktales and tradition of his area. 'I heard most of the stories from Michael McLoughlin of Guberveeny (Killinag Parish). Had I known that one day someone like yourself would come recording them I could have heard three times as many. I was only a young man when I first heard them.'

Tales Nos 15, 16, 22, 56, 68.

Tom Trainor

Aged 65 years in 1956. Carrickmacstay, Clonallon Parish, Co Down. Farmer and autioneer. Has a wide knowledge of the folk beliefs in the area.

Tale No 76.

The storytellers : Frank 'Wings' Campbell

Scope and arrangement of the notes
This collection is not aimed mainly at scholars, but it has been felt that the following notes will increase its usefulness for comparative folkloristic research as well as being of some interest to the layman who wants to know something about the tales.

Under each Tale Number the source and method of collecting have first been given. The stories in this book have been collected in three different ways:

1. Some of the tales have been written down especially for this collection as the collector remembers having heard them long ago. Many of these stem from his father and mother; in other cases it has not always been possible to name the storytellers, and then only the area where he heard these tales has been given. All the tales in category 1 have been denoted by the phrase *written down as the collector remembers it*, or *written down as the collector remembers having heard it.*

2. Other tales have been taken down in writing from the storytellers either while they actually told their stories or immediately afterwards. As a rule these tales have also soon afterwards been checked with the storytellers Tales belonging to this category have been designated *taken down.*

3. Still other tales have been recorded on tape. In such cases the tapes as well as the transcriptions are archived in the Department of Irish Folklore, University College, Dublin. The phrase *recorded* has been used about tales in this category.

Whenever it has been necessary to talk about the material without indicating by what method it was brought together the term *collected* has been used.

Material collected by Michael J Murphy in his capacity of full-time collector for the Irish Folklore Commission or, since the Commission was wound up on 1 April 1971, for the Department of Irish Folklore, University College, Dublin - which carries on the work of the Commission - has been designated *IFC.* The number following this signum refers to the manuscripts in the Department's Archives. Recent, as yet unbound and unpaginated manuscripts, which have not been indexed, have been referred to as *IFC n.i.**

The month and year of collection and the name and county of the storyteller have been given wherever possible. Further information about the storytellers can be found in the foregoing section of notes, p. 150. In that list, Michael J Murphy himself is given as the informant in the case of tales in group 1, but wherever it has been possible to nail the source to particular individuals, they have also been listed under his or her name within round brackets.

As a helpful measure to those who would like to investigate the distribution of tales in the North of Ireland, references to other variants collected by Michael J Murphy have also been given. This comparative material has not

* It has not been possible to trace the manuscript numbers of some of the tales, known to be included in the Archives of the Department of Irish Folklore. These tales are Nos. 8, 10, 13, 22, 26, 31, 51, 55, 63 and 101. These tales have been printed from carbon copies in Michael J Murphy's custody.

been listed in the index of storytellers. It must also be stressed that the lack of such other variants under any particular Tale Number is not a guarantee that Michael J Murphy has not collected other variants, nor is the inclusion of one or several other variants a guarantee that he may not have collected others. The material Michael J Murphy has sent in to the Commission and the Department over the years now amounts to some 24,000 pages and it has not been possible to go through all of it in connection with the editing of this book.

For many reasons it has been necessary to restrict further notes on the stories to a bare minimum. Scholars are likely to deplore many omissions and oversights here, but it is nevertheless hoped that they will find it better to have, rather than to be without, the pieces of information given. The ordinary reader may also want to find other versions of one or the other of the stories in this book and for this reason references to some easily available standard collections of Irish tales have been given. These references may also serve as a guide for further reading. The following works have been used:

1. Antti Aarne & Stith Thompson, *The Types of the Folktale* (Second Revision, Helsinki 1961 = *FF Communications* 184). References are given to Type Numbers, which as a rule are the same as those in *The Types of the Irish Folktale* (see next item). Whenever it has been necessary to distinguish this former work from the latter, *The Types of the Folktale* has been referred to as *AT*. The inclusion of a story in *AT* will in most cases indicate that it is an international tale, found in more than one country in Europe, frequently almost everywhere between Ireland and India and occasionally even further afield. *AT* also includes full bibliographical notes on each tale.

2. Seán Ó Súilleabháin & Reidar Th. Christiansen, *The Types of the Irish Folktale* (Helsinki 1963 = *FF Communications* 188). References have been given to Type Numbers. Whenever it has been necessary to distinguish this work from *The Types of the Folktale* it has been referred to as *IT*. This work consists of a list of Irish versions of international folktales in print and manuscript up to the year 1956. Whenever variants appearing in this book or mentioned in the notes are not included in *IT* - either because they have been collected after 1956 or because they have been overlooked in the process of indexing - this has been adverted to below, through the statement 'the above variant to be added to those listed in *IT*', or some such phrase.

3. Stith Thompson, *Motif-Index of Folk-literature* (Rev. and enlarged ed., Copenhagen 1955-58). Reference has been given to *Motif*. Since motifs are registered in *AT* as well as in some of the works below, references have only been given in cases of special interest, whenever the information is not readily available elsewhere.

4. Frederic C. Tubach, *Index Exemplorum, A Handbook of Medieval Religious Tales* (Helsinki 1969 = *FF Communications* 204). A list with bibliographical references to tales used by preachers in the Middle Ages to enliven their sermons. Many such *exempla* have found their way into folk tradition, not least in Ireland. This work is quoted *Tubach*.

5. Seán Ó Súilleabháin, *Scéalta Cráibtheachta* (*Béaloideas* 21, 1951). The

most comprehensive collection of Irish holy legends. The tales are in the Irish language but the book contains an English summary where Type Numbers and Motifs are given. This work is cited *SC.*

6. Sean O'Sullivan, *Folktales of Ireland* (London 1966). A collection of Irish folktales in English translation with index of Type Numbers and Motifs with full notes. Quoted *FTI.*

7. Sean O'Sullivan, *The Folklore of Ireland* (London 1974). Contains mainly folktales. Annotated in the same way as *FTI.* Quoted *FLI.*

8. Séamus Ó Duilearga, *Leabhar Scáin Í Chonaill. Sgéalta agus Seanchas ó Íbh Ráthach* (Baile Atha Cliath 1948, 2nd ed. Baile Atha Cliath 1964). In Irish but with English summary and full comparative notes, including Type Numbers and Motifs.

Other sources referred to in the comparative notes, mostly such as cannot be reached through the works listed above, have been quoted in full.

In a few cases early occurrences of the tales in medieval and classical sources have been pointed out in the notes. No strict principles have been followed here. These pieces of information, however, may be of interest to students of literature and it has also been thought likely to be of some value for the general reader to see that even such stories as may appear quite modern at first glance may have entertained people hundreds and even thousands of years ago.

That there is also good hope for the survival of many tales in the future is indicated by the fact that quite a number of them have been included in popular joke books published within the last few years. Some examples of this have been given. Finally it ought to be stressed that the fact that no parallels have been quoted for certain stories does not necessarily indicate that these are unique or even especially rare. It shows, rather that collectors as well as scholars have given little attention to certain types of stories, for instance such humorous tales as have not been included in *AT.* It is to be hoped that this little collection may help in focusing attention on such neglected story genres, which are of no less importance than the better known ones in deepening our understanding of what people enjoy and peoples' outlook on life.

Confession Tales (Nos 1 - 7)

1. 'Anchor There'

Written down as the collector remembers it from his father, Michael Murphy, Co Armagh.

Jokes and anecdotes about confession, such as Nos 1 - 7 in this collection, are extremely popular in the North as well as elsewhere in Ireland. The category is not included in *AT*, but many stories of this kind are listed in *IT* under Type 1811, 'Jokes about Religious Vows'. Cf also Type 1810, 'Jokes about Catechism'.

2. Peas as Penance

Written down as the collector remembers having heard it in Co Armagh and elsewhere.

3. 'Two Days Running and Skip One'

IFC 1621, p 113. Taken down in March 1963 from James Loughran, Co Louth.

A variant of this anecdote is found in Michael Kilgariff, *More Best Religious Jokes* (London 1974), p. 24.

4. 'Who Made Me?'

IFC 974, p. 344 - 345. Taken down in August 1943 from the collector's father, Michael Murphy, Co Armagh. Another variant taken down by Michael J Murphy in March 1945 from Stephen Fitzpatrick, Co Down in *IFC* 975, p. 632 - 633.

Type 1810, 'Jokes about Catechism'. Both the above variants to be added to those listed in *IT.*

5. A Bag of Begods

Written down as the collector remembers having heard it in Co Armagh. Another variant taken down by Michael J Murphy in August 1943 from Myles Mallon, Co Armagh, in *IFC* 974, p. 343 - 344.

6. He Stole a Bit of Old Rope

Written down as the collector remembers it from his father, Michael Murphy, Co Armagh.

Type 1800, 'Stealing Only a Small Amount'. The above variant to be added to those listed in *IT.*

7. The Man Who Stole a Ham

IFC 1566, p. 216 - 217. Taken down in February 1960 from Dan Rooney, Co Down. Other variants taken down by Michael J Murphy in *IFC* 1112, p. 172 (October 1945 from Mary Daly, Co Louth), *IFC* 1113, p. 12 (January 1946 from Paddy O'Hare, Co Armagh) and *IFC* 1113, p. 458 (July 1948 from the collector's father, Michael Murphy, Co Armagh).

Type 1807A, 'Owner has Refused to Accept it'. Dan Rooney's and Mary Daly's versions to be added to those listed in *IT.*

Tales of Priest and Parson (Nos 8 - 16)

8. In the Dark

Taken down c 1963 from James Loughran, Co Louth. Other variants taken down by Michael Murphy in *IFC* 975, p. 629 - 630 (March 1945 from Stephen Fitzpatrick, Co Down) and *IFC* 1566, p. 184 - 185 (February 1960 from Dan Rooney, Co Down).

Types 1810A*, 'How Many Gods are There?' + 1833E, 'God Died for You' + 1832N*, 'Lamb of God Becomes Sheep of God'.

9. The Priest to be Silenced

IFC 1568, p. 53 - 54. Taken down in September 1961 from James Loughran, Co Louth. Another version taken down by Michael Murphy in February 1942 from his father, Michael Murphy, Co Armagh, in *IFC* 974, p. 72.

Motif V43, 'Holy man has his own mass'. Cf. Type 759B, 'Holy Man Has his own Mass' and *SC* No 106.

10. The Dog That Wouldn't Eat Meat on a Friday

Taken down c 1963 from James Loughran, Co Louth. Other variants collected by Michael J Murphy in *IFC* 1560, p 187 (taken down in February 1960 from Dan Rooney, Co Down) and *IFC n.i.* (recorded in July 1975 from Michael Rooney, Co Cavan).

Versions of this story have been listed in *IT* under Type 1530*, 'The Man and his Two Dogs'. All the above variants to be added to those listed in *IT*. If this story is to be taken as a byform of that included in *AT*, it offers a striking example of how even the most profane stories may take on a religious colouring in Irish tradition (cf Bo Almqvist in *Studia Hibernica* 4, 1964, p 215).

11. The Dead Priest Speaks

IFC 974, p. 17 - 18. Taken down in January 1942 from James McCann, Co Armagh. Another variant taken down by Michael J Murphy in March 1945 from Ketty Courtney, Co Down, in *IFC* 925, p. 544.

12. Old Thorns and Old Priests are to be Feared

Written down as the collector remembers having heard it in Co Armagh and elsewhere. Another variant taken down by Michael J Murphy in May 1962 from James Loughran, Co Louth, in *IFC* 1570, p. 168.

13. The Power of the Priest

Taken down in 1945 from Stephen Fitzpatrick, Co Down.

14. For the Good of Her Ass

Written down as the collector remembers it from his father, Michael Murphy, Co Armagh.

15. The Greedy Priest and the Tramp

IFC n.i. Recorded in June 1974 from Michael Rooney, Co Cavan. Cf Type 1704, 'Anecdotes about Absurdly Stingy Persons'.

16. 'It Died a Protestant'

IFC n.i. Recorded in September 1974 from Michael Rooney, Co Cavan.

17. The Three Questions

Written down as the collector remembers it from his father, Michael Murphy, Co Armagh. Printed in *Ulster Folklife* 19 (1973), p. 34 - 35. Other variants collected by Michael J Murphy in *IFC* 974, p. 108 (taken down in February 1942 from Barney O'Hare, Co Armagh), *IFC* 974, p. 143 (taken down in February 1942 from Tom Dunne, Co Armagh), *IFC* 975, p. 731 (taken down in April 1945 from Stephen Fitzpatrick, Co Down), *IFC n.i.* (recorded in July 1973 from Michael McGovern, Co Cavan) and *IFC n.i.* (recorded in September 1974 from Michael Rooney, Co Cavan).

Type 922, 'The Shepherd Substituting for the Priest Answers the King's Questions'. All the above variants, except Stephen Fitzpatrick's, to be added to those listed in *IT.* For this tale see, in addition to the references in *AT*, Alan Bruford, ' "The King's Questions" (*AT* 922) in Scotland' in *Scottish Studies* 17 (1973), p. 147 - 154 and Edwin C. Kirkland, 'The American Redaction of Tale Type 922' in *Fabula* 4 (1961), p. 248 - 263.

See furthermore *LSC* No 33.

18. Three Things God Can't Do

Written down as the collector remembers it from Francis McBride, Co Tyrone.

Cf Vernam Hull and Archer Taylor, *A Collection of Irish Riddles* (Berkley & Los Angeles 1955), No 489.

19. The Wee Red Moiley

Written down as the collector remembers it from Dan Rooney, Co Down. Other variants taken down by Michael J Murphy in *IFC* 975, p. 259 (January 1945 from Felix O'Hanlon, Co Down) and *IFC* 1570, p. 168 (May 1962 from James Loughran, Co Louth).

20. The Breed of the Old Mare

Written down as the collector remembers having heard it in Co Antrim.

Motifs G241.2.1, 'Witch transforms man to horse and rides him', and G211.1.1.2, 'Witch as horse shod with horse-shoes'.

21. 'I Won't Lay a Tooth on Her'

Written down as the collector remembers it from his father, Michael Murphy, Co Armagh.

22. A Hungry Hired Boy

IFC n.i. Recorded in 1973 from Michael Rooney, Co Cavan.

23. 'Go On With the Funeral'

IFC 974, p. 311 - 312. Taken down in March 1943 from the collector's father, Michael Murphy, Co Armagh.

24. A Boy Named Abraham

Written down as the collector remembers it from his father, Michael Murphy, Co Armagh. Other variants collected by Michael J Murphy in *IFC* 1112, p. 169

(taken down in October 1945 from Mary Daly, Co Louth) and *IFC* 1570, p. 161 (taken down in April 1962 from James Loughran, Co Louth).
IT 1833**, 'Other Anecdotes of Sermons'.

25. 'How Do You Like Your Egg Boiled?'
Written down as the collector remembers it from Michael E Morris, Co Tyrone. Another variant taken down by Michael J Murphy in July 1948 from his father, Michael Murphy, Co Armagh, in *IFC* 1113, p. 456.

Husband and Wife Tales (Nos 26 - 35)

26. The 'Dead' Husband Returns
Recorded in 1972 from Phill McDonnell, Co Cavan. Printed in *Ulster Folklife* 19 (1973), p. 31 - 33. Another variant taken down by Michael J Murphy in January 1942 from his father, Michael Murphy, Co Armagh, in *IFC* 974, p. 27 - 28.
Type 1792A, 'The Priest's Pig'. Both the above variants to be added to those listed in *IT*. 'The Priest's Pig' is a special development, particularly popular in Ireland, of a tale - Type 1792, 'The Stingy Parson and the Slaughtered Pig' - well attested on the Continent in the Middle Ages. It is found, for instance, in Boccaccio's *Decameron* (VIII: 6).

27. 'I Wish Death Would Take Me'
Written down as the collector remembers having heard it in Co Armagh and elsewhere. Another variant taken down by Michael J Murphy in September 1943 from his father, Michael Murphy, Co Armagh, in *IFC* 974, p. 363.
Type 1354, 'Death for the Old Couple'. In *IT* some of the variants have also been listed under Type 845, 'Old Man and Death'. Both the above variants to be added to those listed in *IT*.

28. A Desperate Falling Out
IFC 1566, p. 167. Taken down in February 1960 from Dan Rooney, Co Down. Printed in *Ulster Folklife* 11 (1965), p. 85.
Cf Type 1380, 'The Faithless Wife'. The 'marrow-bone' or 'milk-toast motif' is lacking in this variant but it seems likely, nevertheless, that it is related to Type 1380. For a very similar variant see Séamas Ó Catháin and Patrick O'Flanagan, *The Living Landscape, Kilgalligan, Erris, County Mayo* (Dublin 1975), p. 137 - 139.

29. The Travelling Woman and the Sowans
IFC 1566, p. 171 - 172. Taken down in February 1962 from Dan Rooney, Co Down. Printed in *Ulster Folklife* 11 (1965), p. 85 - 86.
Type 1423, 'The Enchanted Pear Tree'. Both the above variants to be added to those listed in *IT*. The tale was popular in the Middle Ages. It occurs for instance in Boccaccio's *Decameron* (VII: 9) and Chaucer's *Canterbury*

Tales ('Merchant's Tale'). See, in addition to reference in *AT*, Charles A Watkins, 'Modern Irish Variants of the Enchanted Pear Tree' in *Southern Folklore Quarterly* (1966), p. 201 - 213. See also *SC* No 8 and *Tubach* No 3265.

30. Beyond Redemption

Written down as the collector remembers having heard it in Co Antrim. Another variant taken down by Michael J Murphy in July 1955 from Alec Anderson, Co Antrim, in *IFC* 1390, p. 157.

31. A Divil's Imp of a Woman

Taken down c 1960 from Dan Rooney, Co Down. Another variant taken down by Michael J Murphy in January 1962 from James Loughran, Co Louth, in *IFC* 1569, p. 19.

32. The Woman has the Last Word

IFC 1220, p. 280 - 281. Taken down in June 1951 from Pat Crangle, Co Down. Another variant taken down by Michael J Murphy in November 1963 from James Loughran, Co Louth, in *IFC* 1569, p. 6 - 7.

Type 1365B, 'Cutting with the Knife or the Scissors'. Pat Crangle's variant to be added to those listed in *IT*. Used as an *exemplum* in the Middle Ages; see for instance T F Crane, *The Exempla of Jacques de Vitry* (London 1890), No 221.

33. Courtship and Marriage

A. Written down as the collector remembers having heard it in Co Armagh.
B. Written down as the collector remembers having heard it in Co Cavan.
C. Written down as the collector remembers having heard it in Co Armagh.
See Vernam Hull and Archer Taylor, *A Collection of Irish Riddles*, No 649.

34. Pigs Can Go Under a Big Pot

IFC 1566, p. 179. Taken down in February 1960 from Dan Rooney, Co Down.

35. 'More Cake or I'll Appear'

Written down as the collector remembers having heard it in Co Armagh. James G Delaney, full-time collector, Hudson Bay, Athlone, reports that he has heard this story in his district (oral communication).

The Clever and the Foolish (Nos 36 - 51)

36. The Clever Man and the Fool

IFC 1566, p. 133 - 138. Taken down in January 1960 from Dan Rooney, Co Down. Printed in *Ulster Folklife* 11 (1965), p. 81 - 84.

Type 1539, 'Cleverness and Gullibility'. The above variant to be added to those listed in *IT*.

37. The Blacksmith and the Tailor

A & B written down as the collector remembers them from Patrick McCullagh, Co Tyrone. Another variant taken down by Michael J Murphy in January 1945 from James Morgan, Co Down, in *IFC* 975, p. 236 - 237.

B is Type 1631*, 'The Tailor and the Smith as Rivals'. The tale has not earlier been noted in Irish tradition. *AT* lists variants from Estonia and Lithuania.

38. A Wind-Broken Woman

IFC 1619, p. 269 - 270. Taken down in June 1961 from James Loughran, Co Louth.

Type 501, 'The Three Old Women Helpers'. The above variant to be added to those listed in *IT*. It is interesting to note how all the supernatural motifs ordinarily found in this Type have been obliterated in James Loughran's variant.

39. 'Had Your Agent Horns?'

IFC 1619, p. 268. Taken down in May 1961 from James Loughran, Co Louth. Another variant taken down by Michael J Murphy in March 1945 from Stephen Fitzpatrick, Co Down, in *IFC* 975, p. 648 - 649.

Type 1600, 'The Fool as Murderer'.

40. The Man Who Lost an Eye

IFC 1622, p. 34 - 35. Taken down in June 1963 from James Loughran, Co Louth.

This tale is not included in *AT*, but many Irish variants are listed in *IT* under Type 155, 'The Ungrateful Serpent Returned to Captivity'. The above variant to be added to those listed there. The same story is to be found in a French 13th century *fabliau*, *D'un Preudome qui rescolt son compere de noier*; English translation in Peter Rickard and others, *Medieval Comic Tales* (Cambridge 1972), p. 2 - 3. See also A Micha, 'A propos d'un fabliau' in *Le Moyen Age* 50 (1949), p. 17 - 20.

41. Unity is Strength

IFC 1622, p. 53. Taken down in July 1963 from James Loughran, Co Louth.

Type 910F, 'The Quarrelling Sons and the Bundle of Twigs'. The above variant to be added to those listed in *IT*. The story is found in Aesop's *Fables*.

42. Half a Blanket

IFC 1623, p. 73. Taken down in November 1963 from James Loughran, Co Co Louth.

Type 980A, 'The Half-Carpet'. The above variant to be added to those listed in *IT*. Common in medieval literature, for instance as an *exemplum*. See T F Crane, *The Exempla of Jacques de Vitry* (London 1890), No 260.

43. Father and Son

Written down as the collector remembers having heard it in Co Tyrone. Story similar to the preceding one.

44. 'You're a Liar!'

IFC 1566, p. 165 - 166. Taken down in February 1960 from Dan Rooney, Co Down.

Type 852, 'The Hero Forces the Princess to Say, "That is a Lie." ' This variant to be added to those listed in *IT.* Found in the Middle Ages, for instance in a Latin poem, *Modus florum*, composed in Germany in the 10th century. See also *FTI* No 53.

45. 'Brigid Bucked Him'

IFC 1570, p. 164 - 166. Taken down in April 1962 from James Loughran, Co Louth.

Type 1305C, 'Miser Would Drink Molten Gold'. This variant to be added to those listed in *IT. AT* only lists Irish instances.

46. Whang the Miller Makes a Match

IFC n.i. Recorded in March 1974 from Myles Dolan, Co Cavan.

Type 1691, ' "Don't Eat too Greedily" '. This Type is not included in *IT*, but our tale is listed there under Type 1775, 'The Hungry Parson'. The above variant to be added to those listed in *IT.*

47. The Fool Who Excaped From Hell

Written down as the collector remembers having heard it in Co Armagh. Another variant taken down by Michael J Murphy in August 1942 from his father, Michael Murphy, Co Armagh in *IFC* 974, p.290.

Type 835A*, 'Drunk Man in the Mine'. In *IT* a number of variants of this story are also found under Type 1833**, 'Other Anecdotes of Sermons'.

48. A Mighty Pick

Written down as the collector remembers having heard it in Co Armagh. Another variant taken down by Michael J Murphy in March 1963 from James Loughran, Co Louth, in *IFC* 1621, p.106.

Type 1960Z, 'Other Stories of Great Objects and the Like'. The above variants to be added to those listed in *IT.*

49. The Lazy Daughter

IFC 1622, p 50 - 52. Taken down in July 1963 from James Loughran, Co Louth.

Type 901, 'Taming of the Shrew'; this variant to be added to those listed in *IT.* Shakespeare founded his well-known comedy on this story. It has often been treated in verse and prose in the Middle Ages. See also *LSC* No 31.

50. The King Who Had to Cry 'Quit!'

IFC 1483, p 237 - 239. Taken down in January 1957 from Peadar Barry, Co Down.

Type 2301A, 'Making the King Lose Patience'. In *IT* this variant is listed under Type 2300, 'Endless Tales'.

51. He Came on the Lord's Daughter A-Drowning

Taken down c 1963 from James Loughran, Co Louth.

A *chantefable.* See F J Child, *The English and Scottish Popular Ballads* (Boston and New York 1882 - 1894), No 46 'Captain Wedderburn's Courtship' cf also No 1 'Riddles Wisely Expounded'. See furthermore Hugh Shields, 'Old British Ballads in Ireland' in *Folk Life* 10 (1972), p 87 - 89.

52. Dan O'Connell and the Eldest Twin

Taken down in September 1963 from Annie Lynch, Co Louth.

Cf Motif H255, 'Test: which of twins is elder'. For Daniel O'Connell in Irish folk tradition see Caoimhín O Danachair, 'Dónall Ó Conaill i mBéal na nDaoine' in *Studia Hibernica* 14 (1974), p 40 - 66.

53. Dan O'Connell Meets His Match

Written down as the collector remembers having heard it in Co Armagh.

Type 1585, 'The Lawyer's Mad Client'. The story forms the basis of the medieval French comedy, *Maistre Pathelin.*

54. Dan O'Connell: A Son of His Da's

Written down as the collector remembers having heard it in Co Armagh. Another variant taken down by Michael J Murphy in March 1943 from Tom Dunne, Co Armagh, in *IFC* 974, p 299.

55. Dan Teaches Ireland How to Whistle

Taken down c 1960 from Dan Rooney, Co Down. Another version taken down by Michael J Murphy in April 1962 from James Loughran, Co Louth, in *IFC* 1570, p 135.

56. Dan Told Him to Sow Peas

Recorded in 1973 from Michael Rooney, Co Cavan. Not yet in *IFC.*

Type 821B, 'Chickens from Boiled Eggs'. This Type is not included in *IT*, but there are several other Irish variants. A study is forthcoming in *Béaloideas.* The story was known in India and elsewhere in the Orient as early as the 5th century.

57. Redmond O'Hanlon and the Servant Boy

IFC 1570, p 72 - 73. Taken down in June 1962 from James Loughran, Co Louth. Another version taken down by Michael J Murphy in February 1942 from James McCann, Co Armagh, in *IFC* 974, p 125 - 127.

The story could fit in under Type 968, 'Miscellaneous Robber and Murder. Stories', but this number is not included in *IT.* Many versions listed in *LSC* No 46.

58. Redmond's Proof of Shot Shirt

Written down as the collector remembers having heard it in Co Down.

Another version taken down by Michael J Murphy in March 1945 from Stephen Fitzpatrick, Co Down, in *IFC* 975, p 613.

59. Dean Swift Finds a Clever Boy

A. *IFC* 975, p 727. Taken down in April 1945 from Stephen Fitzpatrick, Co Down.

Type 875, 'The Clever Peasant Girl'. The above version added to those listed in *IT.* For Jonathan Swift in folk tradition see Mackie L Jarrell, 'Jack and the Dean: Swift Traditions in Ireland' in *Journal of American Folklore* 77 (1964), p 99 - 117. See also *LSC* No 32: II - III.

B. Taken down as the collector remembers having heard it in Co Louth.

Type 785A, 'The Goose with One Leg'. The above version to be added to those listed in *IT.* For Irish variants see also Type 921 in *IT.*

60. Dean Swift Meets a Lawyer's Funeral

A. Taken down as the collector remembers having heard it in Co Louth.
B. Taken down as the collector remembers having heard it in Co Armagh.

Wanderers and Tramps (Nos 61 - 71)

61. The Fenian Secrets

IFC 1390, p 319. Taken down in July 1955 from Johnny Kelly, Co Antrim.

Type 1360B, 'Flight of the Woman and her Lover from the Stable'. The above variant to be added to those listed in *IT*.

62. The Three Advices

IFC 1566, p 123 - 127. Taken down in January 1960 from Dan Rooney, Co Down. Other versions collected by Michael J Murphy in *IFC* 975, p 734 - 735 (taken down in April 1945 from Stephen Fitzpatrick, Co Down), *IFC* 1112, p 140 - 141 (taken down in October 1945 from Mary Daly, Co Louth) and *IFC n.i.* (recorded in April 1973 from Myles Dolan, Co Cavan).

Type 910B, 'The Servant's Good Counsels'.

All the above versions except that in *IFC* 975, p 734 to be added to those listed in *IT*. See furthermore *Tubach* No 4111.

63. The Gallows Thief

Taken down c 1963 from James Loughran, Co Louth. Other variants taken down by Michael J Murphy in *IFC* 974, p 270 (March 1942, from James McCann, Co Armagh) and in *IFC* 975, p 733 (April 1945 from Stephen Fitzpatrick, Co Down).

Type 1525, 'The Master Thief'. James Loughran's variant to be added to those listed in *IT*.

64. A Sort of a Clift

IFC 1221, p 307 -310. Taken down in December 1951 from Michael E Morris, Co Tyrone. Another variant taken down by Michael J Murphy in March 1945 from Stephen Fitzpatrick, Co Down, in *IFC* 975, p 619.

Types 1685A, 'The Stupid Son-in-Law' + 1696, ' "What Should I Have Said (Done)?" '. In *IT* both the above variants are listed under Type 1685, 'The Foolish Bridegroom'.

65. They'll Force You To Take Soup

IFC n.i. Recorded in March 1974 from Myles Dolan, Co Cavan.

66. The Tramp and the Foal

IFC 1619, p 276 - 277. Taken down in May 1961 from James Loughran, Co Louth.

This tale has no Type Number in *AT*, but it is listed in *IT* under 1532A, '(Proof of Ownership by a Trick)'. The above variant to be added to those listed in *IT*. See furthermore *FTI* No 50.

67. The Man with the Bar of Gold

Written down as the collector remembers having heard it in Antrim and elsewhere. Another variant taken down by Michael J Murphy in February 1954 from Pat O'Neill, Co Antrim in *IFC* 1363, p 252.

68. The Castle on the Cuiltiagh Mountain

IFC n.i. Recorded in November 1974 from Michael Rooney, Co Cavan.

Types 326A*, 'Soul Released from Torment + 566 'The Three Magic Objects and the Wonderful Fruits (Fortunatus)'. The above variant to be added to those listed in *IT.*

69. Jack and His Talking Cat

IFC 974, p 303. Taken down in March 1943 from Tom Dunne, Co Armagh. Other variants taken down by Michael J Murphy in *IFC* 974, p 152 (March 1943 from his father, Michael Murphy, Co Armagh) and *IFC* 1112, p 413 (November 1945 from Robbie McAlister, Co Armagh).

Type 545B, 'Puss in Boots'. All the above variants to be added to those listed in *IT.*

70. The Tramp and the Ghost

Written down as the collector remembers having heard it in Co Down.

Another variant taken down by Michael J Murphy in July 1963 from James Loughran, Co Down, in *IFC* 1483, p 48.

71. The Widow's Three Sons

IFC n.i. Recorded in June 1974 from Phill McDonnell, Co Cavan.

Type 1000, 'Bargain Not to Become Angry'. The above variant to be added to those listed in *IT.*

Tales of Enchantment and Wonder (Nos 72 - 76)

72. The Enchanted Island

IFC 1365, p 136 - 137. Taken down in August 1956 from Rose McCurdy, Co Antrim.

For enchanted islands in Irish myth and folklore see Thomas Johnson Westropp, 'Brasil and the Legendary Islands of the North Atlantic: Their History And Fable. A Contribution To The "Atlantis" Problem' in *P.R.I.A.* 30, Sect. C, No 8, p 223 - 260.

73. Lig Na Bayste

IFC 1365, p 170. Taken down in August 1955 from Micky Joe Anderson, Co Antrim.

74. The Woman from the Sea

Written down as the collector remembers having heard it in many places in Co Antrim. Other versions taken down by Michael J Murphy in *IFC* 1365, p 140

(August 1954 from Rose McCurdy, Co Antrim) and *IFC* 1360, p 24 - 26 (January 1953 from Dan Hyndman, Co Antrim).

Many hundred variants of this legend have been collected in Ireland. Some of them are listed in *IT* under Type 1889H, 'Submarine Otherworld'. See also *FLI* No 21, *LSC* No 123 and Reidar Th. Christiansen, *The Migratory Legends* (Helsinki 1958 = *FF Communications* 175), No 4080.

75. Visions of a Murder

IFC 1365, p 158 - 159. Taken down in August 1955 from Micky McCuaig, Co Antrim.

76. The Water Horse of Burren

IFC 1470, p 287. Taken down in September 1956 from Thomas Trainor, Co Down.

Warriors and Giants (Nos 77 - 83)

77. Oisin and St Patrick

Written down as the collector remembers having heard it in Co Armagh.

This story is often found in combination with the tale about Oisin and St Patrick's housekeeper (see Gerard Murphy in *Duanaire Finn* III, Dublin 1953, p xix - xxi). A version from Co Tyrone in Éamonn Ó Tuathail, *Sgéalta Mhuintir Luinigh* (Dublin 1933), No xxxvi.

78. Oisin and The Magic Bull

Written down as the collector remembers having heard it in Co Armagh. Another version taken down by Michael J Murphy in July 1945 from Mary Daly, Co Louth, in *IFC* 974, p 465 - 466.

See Gerard Murphy, *op cit* p xix, note 3.

79. Finn McCool and The Scotch Giant

Written down as the collector remembers having heard it in Co Armagh.

For other variants see Gerard Murphy, *op cit*, p xvi.

80. Finn McCool and the Cailleach Bhiorra

Written down as the collector remembers having heard it in Co Armagh.

81. A Meeting of Two Giants

IFC 1622, p 37. Taken down in June 1963 from James Loughran, Co Louth.

Motif K1951.1, 'Boastful fly-killer'.

82. He Made the Giants Fight

IFC n.i. Recorded in March 1974 from Myles Dolan, Co Cavan.

Motif K1082, 'Ogres (large animals, sharp-elbowed women) duped into fighting each other' + Types 1052, 'Deceptive Contest in Carrying a Tree — Riding' + 1045, 'Pulling the Lake Together' + 1115, 'Attempted Murder with Hatchet'. To be added to the variants listed in *IT*.

83. A Terrible Strong Man

IFC 1390, p 235. Taken down in July 1955 from Frank Craig, Co Antrim. Compare the Old Irish hero tale about the death of Cuchulain.

The Black Art (Nos 84 - 86)

84. Harry Stotle's Black Book

Written down as the collector remembers having heard it in Co Armagh. Another version taken down by Michael J Murphy in November 1945 from Mary Daly, Co Louth, in *IFC* 1112, p 342.

'Harry Stotle' (Aristotle) is a well-known figure in Irish folklore. Stories about 'the black book' (cf Reidar Th. Christiansen, *The Migratory Legends*, Nos 3000 - 3025), however, are uncommon in Irish tradition and the few instances so far recorded seem to be mainly from the North.

85. The Horn Was Off the Cow

IFC 1390, p 314 - 318. Taken down in July 1955 from Johnny Kelly, Co Antrim. Printed in *Ulster Folklife* 3 (1957), p 47 - 48.

86. Rising a Wind Off Rathlin

IFC 1390, p 66. Taken down in June 1955 from Neil Craig, Co Antrim. Motif D2142.1.2, 'Wind raised by loosing certain knots'.

Tales About the Devil (Nos 87 - 94)

87. The Divil's Own Cow

IFC 1568, p 68. Taken down in September 1961 from James Loughran, Co Louth.

88. The Travelling Woman and the Divil

IFC 1566, p 168 - 170. Taken down in February 1960 from Dan Rooney, Co Down. Printed in *Ulster Folklife* 11 (1965), p 84.

Type 1353, 'The Old Woman as Trouble Maker'. The above version to be added to those listed in *IT.* Found in early Indian collections and very popular in the Middle Ages on the Continent. See *Tubach* No. 5361.

89. The Lawyer and the Divil

IFC 1215, p 254 - 255. Taken down in January 1950 from Michael E Morris, Co Tyrone.

Type 1187, 'Meleager'. This mythological motif has been treated by many writers in classical antiquity.

90. Banagher Beats the Divil

IFC 1570, p 167. Taken down in March 1962 from James Loughran, Co Louth.

Type 1030, 'The Crop Division'. Cf *Tubach* No 1921.

91. 'I Thought You Were the Parish Priest'

Written down as the collector remembers it from his father, Michael Murphy, Co Armagh.

92. Married to His Sister

Written down as the collector remembers having heard it in Co Armagh.

A variant is to be found in Ken Nixon, *Best Ulster Jokes* (London 1970), p 34 - 35.

93. 'Can I Buy a Divil, Da?'

Written down as the collector remembers it from his father, Michael Murphy, Co Armagh. Another variant recorded by Michael J Murphy in November 1973 from Michael Rooney, Co Cavan in *IFC n.i.*

Type 1678, 'The Boy who had Never Seen a Woman'. The above variants to be added to those listed in *IT*. Occurring in the story of Barlaam and Josaphat, ultimately based on a legendary life of Buddha, as well as in a number of *exempla* and novellas. See *Tubach* No 5365.

94. Willy the Wisp

IFC n.i. Recorded in March 1974 from Myles Dolan, Co Cavan. Printed in *Mullabawn Historical and Folklore Society* 2 (1972). Other versions taken down by Michael J Murphy in *IFC* 1566, p 162 (February 1960 from Dan Rooney, Co Down), *IFC* 1112, p 336 (November 1945 from Patsy Agnew, Co Armagh) and *IFC* 1215, p 252 (February 1950 from Michael E Morris, Co Tyrone).

Type 330A, 'The Smith and the Devil' (Death). Listed in *IT* under Type 330, 'The Smith Outwits the Devil'. The variants from Myles Dolan and Dan Rooney to be added to those listed in *IT*. This wonder tale, which formed the basis for Father Peadar Ó Laoghaire's famous story *Scéal Shéadna* is immensely popular in Ireland. 562 variants are listed in *IT*. See furthermore *LSC* No 16.

The Saints (Nos 95 - 98)

95. Columbcille Curses the Rushes

IFC 1570, p 156. Taken down in April 1962 from James Loughran, Co Louth.

SC No 73.

96. The Woman's Graveyard in Carrickmore [Co Tyrone]

IFC 1215, p 434 - 435. Taken down in February 1950 from Tommy Nugent, Co Tyrone.

The same story is told about the graveyard in Iona. See for instance C F Gordon Cummings, *In the Hebrides* (London 1883), p 90.

97. Columbcille's Bullock

IFC 1215, p 436 - 437. Taken down in February 1950 from Tommy Nugent, Co Tyrone.

Type 750B, 'Hospitality Rewarded'. This Type Number is not included in *IT*, though the story is common in Irish tradition. See *SC* No 66 and Motif E32,

'Resuscitated eaten animal'. The story occurs in many medieval saints' legends, as well as in Old Norse in Snorri Sturluson's *Edda* and it is also found in the Orient. See, in addition to literature quoted in *AT*, Stig Wikander, 'Tors bockar och patriarkernas kalv' in *Arv* 6 (1950), p 90 - 99.

98. Columbcille and the End of the World

IFC 1567, p 125. Taken down in February 1960 from Dan Rooney, Co Down.

Cf Motifs M357, 'Prophecy: world catastrophe' and M364, 'Various prophecies connected with saints (or holy men)'.

Christ and the Apostles (Nos 99 - 104)

99. St Peter and Christ and the Miser

IFC 1569, p 10 - 11. Taken down in January 1962 from James Loughran, Co Louth.

Variants of this story have been included under Type 785 in *IT*. The above variants to be added to those listed there. See furthermore *SC* No 12.

100. The Penitent Thief

Written down as the collector remembers having heard it in Co Antrim. Other variants taken down by Michael J Murphy in *IFC* 1216, p 122 (April 1950 from Michael E Morris, Co Tyrone) and *IFC* 1366, p 323 (June 1954 from Rosie Emerson, Co Antrim).

SC No 19.

101. 'Christ Explains Why Fishermen Drown

101. Christ Explains Why Fishermen Drown

A & B. Taken down in 1950 from Michael E Morris, Co Tyrone.

B is Type 774K, 'Peter Stung by Bees'. In *IT* many variants of this tale have been listed under Type 759, 'God's Justice Vindicated'. The above variant to be added to those listed in *IT*. See furthermore *SC* No 11.

102. Why the Tinker Keeps Travelling

Written down as the collector remembers it from Pat Crangle, Co Down.

Cf *SC* No 2.

103. Christ

Written down as the collector remembers it from his mother, Mary Murphy, Co Armagh. The same pieces of information were taken down by Michael J Murphy in *IFC* 1112, p 121 (October 1945 from Mary Daly, Co Louth) and in *IFC* 1216, p 120 - 121 (April 1950 from Michael E Morris, Co Tyrone).

104. Judas

Written down as the collector remembers it from his mother, Mary Murphy, Co Armagh. Another variant taken down by Michael J Murphy in April 1950 from Michael E Morris, Co Tyrone, in *IFC* 1216, p 123.

Motif A2721.5, 'Tree on which Judas hanged himself cursed'. Cf *SC* No 17.

Paddy the Irishman (Nos 105 - 111)

105. 'Bags of Heat and Bags of Help'

Written down as the collector remembers having heard it in many places in Co Armagh. A variant taken down by Michael J Murphy in February 1942 from his father, Michael Murphy, Co Armagh, in *IFC* 974, p 76.

106. Sentenced to be Hanged

Written down as the collector remembers it from his father, Michael Murphy, Co Armagh. Another variant taken down by Michael J Murphy in April 1950 from Michael E Morris, Co Tyrone, in *IFC* 1216, p 125 - 126.

Type 1587, 'Man Allowed to pick out Tree to be Hanged on'. In *IT* many variants of this tale have also been listed under Type 927, 'Out-riddling the Judge'. This variant to be added to those listed in *IT*. See also *Tubach* No 4790.

107. The Pope's Luggage

Written down as the collector remembers it from his father, Michael Murphy, Co Armagh.

For other anecdotes about people trying to enter Heaven riding piggy-back see Bo Almqvist, 'The Fisherman in Heaven' in *Béaloideas* 39 - 41 (1971 - 1973), p 43.

108. You Want to Change Your Religion

Written down as the collector remembers having heard it in Co Armagh. Another variant taken down by Michael J Murphy in September 1943 from his father, Michael Murphy, in *IFC* 974, p 363.

109. The Flea's Wake

Written down as the collector remembers it from his father, Michael Murphy, Co Armagh.

110. The Bear's Den

Written down as the collector remembers it from his father, Michael Murphy, Co Armagh. Another variant taken down by Michael J Murphy in February 1954 from Pat O'Neill, Co Antrim, in *IFC* 1363, p 256.

111. Paddy at Sea

A & B. Both these anecdotes are written down as the collector remembers them from his father, Michael Murphy, Co Armagh.

Fantastic Tales (Nos 112 - 114)

112. His Westcoat Barked

IFC 1566, p 151. Taken down in January 1960 from Dan Rooney, Co Down. Printed in *Ulster Folklife* 11 (1965), p 85.

Type 1889L**, 'Mittens Chase Deer'. The above variant to be added to those listed in *IT*.

113. A Brave Good Shot

IFC 1215, p 202. Taken down in January 1950 from Francis McBride, Co Tyrone.

Types 1894, 'The Man Shoots a Ramrod Full of Ducks' + 1890, 'The Lucky Shot'.

114. A Bush Grew Out of His Back

IFC 1566, p 141 - 142. Taken down in January 1960 from Dan Rooney, Co Down.

Type 1911A, 'Horse's New Backbone'. Cf. also Type 1889C, 'Fruit Tree Grows from Head of Deer'. The above variant to be added to those listed in *IT.* See furthermore *FTI* No 53, which also contains the 'reaping-hook-in-the-animal' motif, commonly found in Irish versions of Type 852, 'The Hero Forces the Princess To Say, "That is a Lie" ' (cf No 44 above, where, however, this motif is lacking).

Tales of Animals, Birds and Insects (Nos 115 - 130)

115. The Cat and the Mouse in a Public House

Written down as the collector remembers it from Tom Dunne, Co Armagh.

Type 111A*, 'A Drunkard's Promise'. The above variant to be added to those listed in *IT.* Found for instance in the 15th century Spanish collection *Libro de los gatos,* translated in Peter Rickard and Others, *Medieval Comic Tales* (Cambridge 1972), p 39. See furthermore *Tubach* No 3426.

116. A Clever Fox

Written down as the collector remembers having heard it in Co Armagh).Other variants taken down by Michael J Murphy in *IFC* 974, p 320 (July 1943 from Tom Dunne, Co Armagh) and *IFC* 976, p 12 (March 1945 from Michael O'Hare, Co Armagh).

Type 67**, 'Fox Caught by Butcher'. The above variants, except Michael O'Hare's to be added to *IT.* See also *LSC* No 5.

117. The Last Fox on Rathlin Island

Written down as the collector remembers having heard it on Rathlin, Co Antrim.

118. The Cat and the Fox

IFC 1620, p 92. Taken down in October 1962 from James Loughran, Co Louth.

Type 105, 'The Cat's Only Trick'. The above variant to be added to those listed in *IT.*

119. The Fox Rids Himself of Fleas

Written down as the collector remembers having heard it in Co Louth. Other variants taken down by Michael J Murphy in *IFC* 1566, p 157 (January 1960 from Dan Rooney, Co Down) and *IFC* 1622, p 26 (June 1963 from James Loughran, Co Louth).

Type 63, 'The Fox Rids Himself of Fleas'. All the above variants to be added to those listed in *IT.*

120. The Ass and the Bullock

Written down as the collector remembers having heard it in Co Armagh. Another variant taken down by Michael J Murphy from his father, Michael Murphy, Co Armagh, in *IFC* 974, p 56.

Type 207A, 'Ass Induces Overworked Bullock to Feign Sickness'. Both the above variants to be added to those listed in *IT*.

121. The Talking Jackdaw

Written down as the collector remembers having heard it in Co Armagh. Other variants taken down by Michael J Murphy in *IFC* 974, p 58 - 59.(February 1942 from his father, Michael Murphy, Co Armagh) and *IFC* 1569, p 3 - 4 (November 1961 from James Loughran, Co Louth).

122. The Smith and his Ass

IFC 1569, p 79. Taken down in December 1961 from James Loughran, Co Louth. Another variant taken down by Michael J Murphy in March 1945 from Stephen Fitzpatrick, Co Down, in *IFC* 975, p 631.

123. The Weasel's Spit

IFC 1569, p 132. Taken down in January 1962 from James Loughran, Co Louth. Other variants recorded by Michael J Murphy in *IFC* 1804, p 26. (May 1972 from Michael Rooney, Co Cavan) and *IFC n.i.* (March 1974 from Philip Dolan, Co Cavan).

Type 168*, 'The Weasel and the Poison'. All the above variants to be added to those listed in *IT*.

124. Why the Ass Has a Cross on Its Back

Written down as the collector remembers it from his mother, Mary Murphy, Co Armagh.

Motif A2356.2.7, 'Why ass has cross on back (shoulders)'.

125. The Hedgehog Races the Hare

IFC 1622, p 36. Taken down in June 1963 from James Loughran, Co Louth. Another variant collected by Michael J Murphy in March 1974 from Philip Dolan, Co Cavan, in *IFC n.i.*

Type 275A, 'Hare and Tortoise Race: Sleeping Hare'. This Type Number is missing in *IT*, though the tale is fairly common in Ireland.

126. The Robin

IFC 1570, p 148. Taken down in April 1962 from James Loughran, Co Louth.

Motif A2221.2.2, 'Blood from cross on robin redbreast'.

127. The Wren

IFC 1570, p 148 - 149. Taken down in April 1962 from James Loughran, Co Louth.

Type 221, 'The Election of Bird-king'. The above variant to be added to those listed in *IT*.

128. 'Don't Forget Yesterday'

Written down as the collector remembers it from his mother, Mary Murphy, Co Armagh. Other variants taken down by Michael Murphy in *IFC* 1215 (January

1950 from Michael E Morris, Co Tyrone) and *IFC* 1621, p 131 (April 1963 from James Loughran, Co Louth).

Motif A2231.7.1, 'Beetle cursed for betraying Holy Family'. See furthermore *LSC* No 4.

129. Why A Dog's Nose is Always Cold

IFC 1517, p 125. Taken down in February 1960 from Dan Rooney, Co Down.

See Katherine M Briggs, *A Dictionary of British Folk-tales*, Part A:2 (London 1970), p 348.

130. Three Coldest Things in the World

Written down as the collector remembers having heard it in Co Armagh.

For other examples of this triad see for instance Thomas F O'Rahilly, *A Miscellany of Irish Proverbs* (Dublin 1922), No 246 'An Seabhac' (Pádraig Ó Siochfhradha), *Seanfhocail·na Muimhneach* Baile Átha Cliath 1926), No 1322 and Tomás S Ó Maille, *Sean-fhocla Chonnacht* (Baile Átha Cliath 1948 - 52), No 4058.

The Danes

131. The Danes Could Make Wine from Heather

Written down as the collector remembers having heard it from Frank McAuley, Co Antrim.

IT 2412E, '(Danish Heather Beer)'. The above variant to be added to those listed in *IT*. See furthermore *FLI* No 25, *FTI* No 46, *LSC* No 22:II, Bo Almqvist, 'The Viking ale and the Rhine gold' in *Arv* 21 (1965), p 115 - 135 and sources and treatments quoted there.

132. A Wild Bad Day on the Braes of Layde

Written down as the collector remembers having heard it from Frank McAuley, Co Antrim.

Cf *FLI* p 133 - 134.

133. The Danes Own All Ireland

Written down as the collector remembers having heard it from Frank McAuley, Co Antrim.

This seems to be a truncated variant of Type 726*, 'The Dream Visit'. This variant to be added to those listed in *IT*. See furthermore *FTI* No 36 and Reidar Th Christiansen, 'The People of the North' in *Lochlann* 2 (1962), p 137 - 164, *FLI* No 25, *FTI* No 36 and *LSC* No 22: I.

October 1975
Bo Almqvist

INDEX OF TALE TYPES

(Type numbers are from Antti Aarne and Stith Thompson, *The Types of the Folktale* [Second Revision, Helsinki 1961 = *FF Communications* 184]. For type numbers given in round brackets, as well as for Irish versions of all types, see Seán Ó Suilleabháin and Reidar Th Christiansen, *The Types of the Irish Folktale* [Helsinki 1963 = *FF Communications* 188].)

Occasionally there are minor variations in the titles of the tales between *The Types of the Folktale* and *The Types of the Irish Folktale*; in such cases *The Types of the Folktale* has been followed. It should also be noted that some of the tales in this collection are composite and consist of more than one type number.)

1. ANIMAL TALES (1 - 299)

Type No		*Tale No*
63	The Fox Rids himself of Fleas	119
67**	Fox Caught by Butcher	116
105	The Cat's Only Trick	118
111A*	A Drunkard's Promise	115
Cf 155	The Ungrateful Serpent Returned to Captivity	40
168*	(The Weasel and the Poison)	123
207A	Ass Induces Overworked Bullock to Feign Sickness	120
221	The Election of Bird-king	127
275A	Hare and Tortoise Race: Sleeping Hare	125

2. ORDINARY FOLKTALES

A. Tales of Magic (300 - 749)

326A*	Soul Released from Torment	68
330A	The Smith and the Devil (Death)	94
501	The Three Old Women Helpers	38
545B	Puss in Boots	69
566	The Three Magic Objects and the Wonderful Fruits (Fortunatus)	68
726*	The Dream Visit	133

B. Religious Tales (750 - 849)

750B	Hospitality Rewarded	97
Cf 759B	Holy Man Has his own Mass	9
774K	Peter Stung by Bees	101
785A	The Goose with One Leg	59B
821B	Chickens from Boiled Eggs	56
835A*	Drunk Man in the Mine	47

C. Novelle (Romantic Tales 850 - 999)

D. Tales of the Stupid Ogre (1000 - 1199)

3. JOKES AND ANECDOTES (1200 - 1999)